MATT LAWSON

THE UNADJUSTEDS

MARISA NOELLE

The Shadow Keepers

The Unraveling of Luna Forester

The Mermaid Chronicles

Secrets of the Deep

Quest for Atlantis

Fight for Freedom

Ghost Pirates

Vendetta

Denizens of Darkness

Vortex Returns

The Mermaid Chronicles Companion Guide

THE UNADJUSTEDS UNIVERSE

The Unadjusteds Trilogy
The Unadjusteds
The Rise of The Altereds
The Reckoning

Companion Novellas
Silver Melody
Matt Lawson
Joe Rucker
Paige Starling
President Bear
Hal Small
Erica Swiftfield
Kyle Lewis
Jacob Shea
Sawyer Watson
Addison Shields

CONTENT WARNINGS

This book contains themes and references that some readers may find distressing, including, but not limited to:

Violence – Physical fights and injuries.

Death – Characters dying, sometimes in graphic or emotionally intense ways.

Torture/Abuse – Physical or psychological torture or abusive power dynamics.

Oppression – Totalitarian regimes, discrimination, or forced conformity.

Rebellion/Anarchy – Destructive acts, rebellion against authority, or revolution.

Imprisonment/Enslavement – Characters held against their will, enslaved, or confined.

Manipulation/Brainwashing – Mind control or forced ideological conformity.

Mental Health Issues – Depression, PTSD, anxiety.

Body Horror/Mutations – Genetic modifications, experiments, or body mutilations.

To those who dare to dream of a better world, even when everything seems lost.

CHAPTER 1

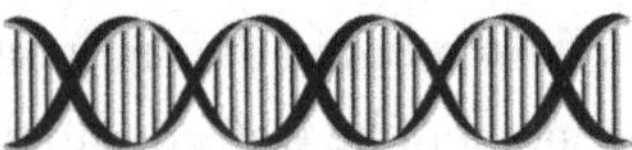

MATT SHOVES the few electronic components he scrounged from his dad's garage workshop into his backpack. He plans to connect them to the explosive devices later and hopes to hell he doesn't blow up the school. Sometimes he wonders if he should have gone down the genetics route, to try to reverse the worst of it. But it's too late now. Modifications have taken root all over the world. There is no going back. The only thing that can be done is to throw a bomb at the whole situation. Metaphorically speaking, of course. But the pun curls his lips into a grim smile.

If only they knew the truth. *They.* That mysterious 'they' behind all the government corruption and corporate greed. The 'they' who would throw him in prison in a cell next to Silver's mother. The 'they' who would end his life if they knew what he was up to.

Two years ago, when his friend died and when Silver's mother was thrown in prison, he never thought he'd be part of a resistance, let alone one of its leaders. But change doesn't happen on its own. You have to take risks. Even if they are dangerous. Even if you're scared. And Matt is scared. Hell, he is terrified. So terrified it's getting hard to face his family every day. To lie to them about the extent of his involvement. But he can't risk their safety by including them in everything he knows. His silence gives them protection. Well, that's what he tells himself. His involvement in the resistance signed all their death warrants the moment he walked into that first meeting.

Matt sighs as he trudges down the stairs, attempting to shake off the morbid thoughts. But it's Silver's birthday. Of course, all the bad memories are going to invade. And he's going to do his best to make sure Silver's bad memories don't overwhelm her today. Starting with the cake.

Matt joins his family in the kitchen for breakfast, where the overwhelming smell is...sugar. His Mom is icing the cake. *The Cake.* The one he begged her to help him make for Silver. To cheer her up. Hopefully.

Matt eyes the childish princess cake as he sticks a finger in the icing bowl and takes a generous lick of pink frosting. "It's the wrong color. Needs to be brighter." He adds more food coloring. Silver hates pink. But this cake has become tradition. And with her mother in prison, there is no one else to make it. They forgot last year, didn't even cross his mind— he won't let that happen again.

His mom smiles at him. "I hope she likes it."

Matt squeezes her shoulder. "She will." *She will.* His heart gives a little lurch.

"I wish Margaret would have shown me how to make this," his mom says as she tucks a loose strand of hair behind her ear, inadvertently dying it pink. "All those frills of the princess dress."

"It's the thought that counts."

His mom laughs. "Says the boy who needs it to be *exactly* the right shade of pink!"

Lyla swivels toward him, her leotard sparkling, her fake butterfly wings far too close to the real thing. Her hair is tied in a bun and sprayed to within an inch of its life. Heavy stage make-up covers her cheeks and eyes. "Why can't she get a store-bought cake like the rest of us?"

Matt raises an eyebrow. "You know she'd never buy an entire cake just to celebrate a birthday on her own. Maybe try having a little understanding, yeah?"

"But why do *you* need to bake her one?"

Matt's cheeks heat. "I'm her best friend." Hell, Matt is her only friend. And she is all Matt needs too.

Lyla gives him a sly smile. "Is that all?"

"Shut up," Matt says. "It's not like that." But it is Silver who makes his breath catch. Silver who makes his stomach flutter. Silver who makes his lungs seize. Silver who fills his dreams with things that will never happen.

"Yeah..." Lyla smirks. "Whatever you say."

His Dad looks up from reading a news article on his phone at the kitchen table. "Leave your brother alone, Lyla. And don't forget your dance shoes. And a snack! You can't do an audition on one piece of unbuttered toast."

"Whatever." Lyla rolls her eyes as she pushes away from the counter and packs her dance bag.

His Mom puts down the spatula, grabs Lyla's arm as she

marches by. Lyla's eyes widen as she stares at their mom. "What? What did I do?"

His mom takes his sister's chin in her hand. The room fills with silent expectation.

"Silver has been through a lot of...shit—"

"I know that." Lyla tries to pull away, but his mom's hand is firm on her chin.

Matt's stomach churns thinking of everything Silver has been through. Of everything they have been through together. And all the crap he could bring down on her.

"Friendship is important," his mom says. "We can't choose our family, but we do choose our friends. And they become our family. *Silver* is our family. And we will do what we can for her. All of us."

"I don't want a pink princess cake when I turn sixteen," Lyla snaps and stalks out of the room.

"Hormones," his dad mutters.

Matt's stomach falls through his feet. He's never heard his mother talk like that. And if Lyla suspects his real feelings for Silver, does his mom know too? Feelings he thought he kept buried inside and well hidden from anyone who cared to glance his way. But he can't help the way he feels, especially with rumors of an enforced nanite program gathering speed. It will grate against all Silver's wounds. Wounds he wishes he could erase, or at the very least, help to heal.

The cake has to be perfect. It's her *sixteenth*.

His mom wipes her hands on her apron and returns to the cake. "Don't worry, the cake will be perfect. I'll bring it over to Silver's apartment after school, right?"

"Right. Okay, thanks. Gotta go. School time." Matt

glances at his youngest sister, Megan, sitting in her wheelchair at the table, one hand spooning cereal into her mouth, the other petting Einstein, their golden retriever. His chest tightens. He loves her so damn much. He loves his family so damn much. And, *fuck it*, he loves Silver too.

Praying for the heat on his cheeks to abate, Matt heads to the door.

"Wait," his mom calls. "What's bulging out of your pockets?"

Matt shoves his hands in his pockets, finds a few more coils of wire, a small Wi-Fi booster, and a voice activated sensor. He leaves the small, wrapped box inside his pocket. "Stuff I need for school."

His mom arches a brow. "Really? Wire clippings and... whatever that thing is are part of your education? Whatever happened to good old-fashioned textbooks?" She reaches for the bundle in his hand, but he snaps his hand back before she can take anything.

"I need that! I'm working on the voice activated sensor for the school fireworks show."

"You and your toys."

"They're not toys!" he says as he grabs his backpack by the front door. And then, as an afterthought, "You wait, one day my toys will save your life."

He hopes that's never the case, but he's terrified it will be.

The morbid thoughts stick to him like glue as he walks through the bright summer sunshine to school. He catches the eyes of a couple unadjusteds, those who have been to a few of the meetings, but none of them give anything away.

Then he spots Silver walking with her guard. Dimples,

she calls him. Not that he has any. On account of the fact that one of the batches of solider nanites made him look more like a troll, incapable of ever smiling. Matt's breath sticks as he falls into step beside her, catching the clean scent of her hair. Something citrusy.

"Morning!" Matt chucks a sarcastic salute at Dimples, who doesn't bother to acknowledge his presence. "Someone's in a good mood today."

"Shh." Silver nudges him. "Don't get it angry. You know what they're like when they're angry. I've already pissed it off once this morning."

Matt raises his eyebrows, wondering what she could possibly do to piss anyone off. But then troll soldiers aren't known for their humor or understanding.

"I guess I'll save your present for later then," Matt says.

"Later." Silver's features soften as the morning sun plays over her face. "Thank you."

"It's about time you caught up to my age and wisdom," Matt says, desperate to see a smile on her face.

Silver laughs and his chest swells. He did that. He made her laugh. Even though she is without her mother on her sixteenth birthday, he made her laugh.

"As long as you don't give me any of that sweet sixteen crap," she says.

"What if it's something you want?"

"If you can magic my ankle cuff away and break my mom out of prison...then I'll put on a tiara and play spin the bottle and whatever else it is teenagers are supposed to do when they turn sixteen." The softness disappears from her face, but she manages to hold on to the smile.

"I wish I could," Matt says quietly. Maybe he can. If everything goes according to plan.

Silver brushes her fingers against his as they walk. "I know."

"I didn't wear a tiara or play spin the bottle on my birthday."

"I remember. Those leftovers your mom brought me from Mimi's were the best pasta I've had all year." She licks her lips. Matt had gone out to celebrate with his family and a few friends. But the one person he'd really wanted to be there wasn't. Silver. Because she was under armed guard and not allowed out of her apartment except to attend school. He'd wanted to see her later that night, be he'd had one of his meetings, and so asked his mom to drop the food around.

Matt clears his throat, attempting to swallow the lump in it before he speaks. "Speaking of food, my mom made you a cake. Pink, with that stupid princess design you like."

Silver gapes at him. "She what...? She didn't have to do that."

Matt slings an arm around her shoulder, relishing the contact. "I think she secretly wants to adopt you. My sisters are driving her nuts."

Silver lets out a low chuckle, whipping the emotion right back up into Matt's throat.

"She's got enough to deal with without my...issues." Silver looks at her feet as they walk.

Matt stops walking, turns her to face him, lifts her chin so her beautiful silver eyes focus on him. "Don't say that. Don't *ever* say that."

"Keep moving." Dimples hurries them along, his hand gripping his assault rifle. *Fucking douchebag.*

Matt and Silver continue walking in silence. As they near the school, Silver says, "Sorry, I didn't mean to bring down the mood."

"You never do."

Before he can say anything else, cheering from the school courtyard snags both their attentions. Matt spots a building crowd, several pumping arms, a few wide eyes. Nothing good ever comes from an impromptu gathering outside the school doors.

"Get it down! Get it down!"

Matt scans the crowd for familiar faces from the resistance movement, receives a couple curt nods of acknowledgement, but there is nothing they can do here. "Stay together, until we know what's going on."

"Get it down! Get it down!"

"It's probably a stupid stunt," Silver says. "One of the contortionists stuck with their legs behind their neck, or something."

"Get it down! Get it down!"

Someone is about to take a nanite. Or already has. It happens at school occasionally. Some people need the confidence of others around them. Others are peer-pressured into it. But he hasn't seen a crowd like this for a while.

With his fingers firmly wrapped around Silver's wrist, Matt leads them through the crowd. They fight their way to the center of the group to find a freshman on his knees, foaming at the mouth, his hands circling his neck, his eyes bulging. *Shit.*

"Someone call an ambulance," Silver shouts. "Now!" She tosses her phone to a girl with pixie ears, then approaches the struggling boy, placing her hands on either side of his face.

Matt follows, his heart heavy in his chest, knowing it's already too late.

"You are not alone," Silver says to the boy. Just like she said to Diana two years ago.

Blood trickles from the boy's nose, staining his fresh, white T-shirt, and he collapses sideways, out of Silver's grasp. Matt darts forward and grabs him before he hits the cement. Lowering him to the ground, he tucks his own sweatshirt under his head.

The pixie girl screams.

"What did he take?" Silver yells at the crowd, the tendons in her neck taut. "Which nanite did he take?"

Matt rolls the boy onto his side as he continues to choke and gurgle. To foam and bleed.

The pixie girl shouts into Silver's cell phone, yelling about help and ambulances and blood and nanites. The crowd quietens as the boy continues to suffer. Matt scans their faces. Those he knows are unadjusted show horror in their eyes. The others, the alts, they're just glad it isn't them.

Silver glances at a fairy—a cheerleader with butterfly wings. "What did he take?"

"Bulk," the fairy replies.

Matt looks at the youthful face of the dying boy. Only a freshman. He wanted to be a football player. Big and strong and immortal. Most kids who play football end up taking a bulk nanite at some point, or they wouldn't be able to continue. But they are expensive. And not everyone can afford them. And there is a bunch of uncut shit on the black market that is a total gamble. Taking one of those is courting certain death. Maybe that's what this kid has done.

The boy chokes, tries to speak, reaches for Silver kneeling in front of him. She holds his hand. Matt watches their hands, wondering if she too is thinking of Diana.

A yellow, sickly foam pours out of his mouth, then his ears and eyes. Matty shudders against the memory. The boy convulses, then falls still. Dead.

It is less than three seconds before conversation swarms through the crowd. Excited chatter. *Fucking alts.*

Matt gets to his feet. There is nothing more they can do. He nudges Silver and guides her to her feet too.

"Just like Diana," Silver whispers, almost breaking him. Some sixteenth birthday this is turning out to be.

Movement snags Matt's attention. Before he can track it, Dimples shoves the butt of his rifle between Silver's shoulder blades. Silver whirls around, glaring at him, but Dimples points her toward the school entrance. Sirens sound and a modified ambulance arrives—large enough to house bulks or fairies with large wingspans. Two elf-like paramedics move in a blur of speed as they approach the dead kid.

"It's too late," Silver says.

Putting himself between her and Dimples, Matt holds her hand, squeezes gently.

The paramedics lift the dead boy and lay him on a gurney. One of them makes the sign of the cross. Matt almost laughs. Dimples points to the school again.

Matt gives Silver's hand one last squeeze. "You go. I'll talk to the medics. I'll find you later."

"Thanks, Matt." She gives him a hug before slipping away.

There isn't much to tell the medics. The boy took a nanite and died. It happens. Some don't take to the change. Others ingest deadly uncut shit. Either way, it's a tragedy. Kids should not be dying. And now that the enforced nanite program is coming...Matt shakes his head as he trudges to the school entrance. He is one person. One sixteen-year-old kid. Can he really make a difference?

CHAPTER 2

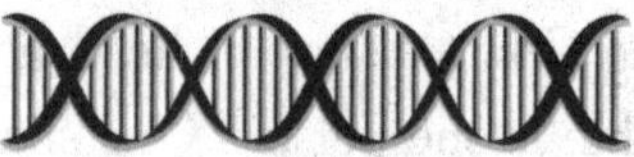

Matt sits at a workbench in the science lab clipping wires and making mental measurements. A handful of other kids surround him; there aren't many in the school who pass the highest levels of scrutiny to gain entry to the most esteemed club—Mr. Arnold's words. The teacher is currently walking around the room and commenting on their individual projects. And yes, one of Matt's projects is a voice activated sensor for the school fireworks show. The other, the one he spends more time on, is far more dangerous. And one that Mr. Arnold is well aware of since he signed up to the resistance movement. He allowed Matt to work on it at school on the condition he didn't blow the building up. Or any of the students.

Matt never thought twice about it. He knows what he's doing. He's ten times smarter than his physics teacher. He just needs to perfect his tools and connection devices. Once school is out for the summer in a couple of weeks, he plans to test it in the forest. Deep in the forest where no one can get hurt.

Matt is about to tidy his equipment and make a move toward homeroom, when the tannoy system screams to life. A couple of kids groan. Then the principal's voice comes over the speaker system.

"Students, please stay where you are and do not proceed to homeroom. We have a special announcement coming up. Teachers, please turn on the monitors wherever you are."

Matt snaps his head up and stares at the speaker, as if he can read what the impending message might be. His gut clenches. He has a feeling he knows. And it's sooner than he expected. Much, much sooner. He is *not* ready.

At the front of the lab, Mr. Arnold switches on a TV monitor. A freshman kid who was forced to take a nanite the day she turned twelve glances at him, her eyes opaque on account of her incredible night vision.

After a moment of darkness and coiling tension, the presidential seal fills the screen...of every channel. The clenching in Matt's stomach moves to his chest, seizing his breath. *Silver. Where is Silver?* In the gym. Karate before school. He has to get to her before all hell breaks loose.

Matt fists his hands as President Bear appears on the screen. Grizzly bear and black widow DNA have turned him into the worst kind of alt. Although he looks human at first glance, his eyes are red, he's overly hairy, and deadly venomous webbing can shoot out of concealed spinnerets on his wrists. That is one alt Matt doesn't want to tangle with. Not that he's much of a fighter to begin with. He's tried to pick up a bit over the last two years since he joined the resistance, knowing he won't always be able to rely on his smarts. But if he's being perfectly honest, he sucks at fighting. His instincts are to talk or run, not throw a punch.

"This is a national announcement," President Bear speaks from the monitor, confirming Matt's suspicions. *"All unadjusteds age twelve and over will now be required to take a nanite pill to enhance their abilities. With threats and competition from overseas, we must do more to further the strength of our country."*

Matt knew it was coming, but he can't help the sharp inhale of breath as the news is delivered. Maybe a part of him believed it wouldn't happen if he wished hard enough.

Chatter among his classmates erupts. A sophomore kid catches his eye. He joined the resistance two weeks ago. Matt shakes his head, a subtle reminder they can't be seen colluding.

"A rep from the nanite representative agency is on its way to every school. They will assign each eligible unadjusted a ticket number," President Bear continues with the announcement that Matt already knows word for word. Francesca worked for the man on his senatorial campaign trail. She has contacts, managed to twist some arms and get a jump start on what was coming down the line. *"You are not permitted to leave before you have your ticket. This ticket will tell you which day within the next two weeks you will be assessed for an appropriate nanite level."*

Mr. Arnold gapes at the TV. Although he is part of the resistance, he has not been given prior knowledge of the announcements. That was only for the leaders—and a handful of people who were the first to spread the word throughout Central City.

"You'll notice some assessments start today. Nanite reps and soldiers are on their way to each school in every city to aid the process," the president continues. *"Once the assessments are complete, we will proceed to residences to evaluate the unadjusted adults. I expect each unadjusted individual to join the strength of the adjusted superbeings. Failure to comply will result in unfortunate circumstances."*

Matt's thoughts fly to Silver. How is she taking this news? Is Claus with her? Kyle? Will they help? Of course they will, he reminds himself, they swore to protect her when Matt isn't around. And to be fair, they are both karate experts—a damn sight more suited to the job than he is.

"Our country is the most powerful in the world. Your loyalty and patriotism are expected. But in case you need a reminder of what happens to traitors..."

Matt stands, every muscle in his body taut.

On the screen, a clip of Silver's mother appears from the day she was arrested. Matt blinks. Then again, trying to rein in his anger. If Silver is watching this...

But more to the point, people will run, and he has to get Silver out of here.

As the chatter in the lab reaches cacophonous proportions, Matt heads to the door.

"Where are you going?" Mr. Arnold asks. "The announcement isn't over."

"Away from here," he says to his teacher, hoping he realizes it's time to run.

Matt darts out of the lab and dashes down the hall,

heading for the comms cupboard to enact the plan he's carried in his head for the last year.

Francesca, his Social Studies teacher and one time campaign assistant to President Bear, grabs his arm as he runs by. She's also the leader of the resistance. "Where are you going?"

"I can't stay here...Silver..."

Francesca checks the hallway. It's empty, for now. "I understand. You know where to go?"

Matt nods.

"And Silver? She knows too?"

"I'm going to tell her now." If he can get on his way.

"We need her." Francesca's serious brown eyes scan his face. "We need her father."

"I know." Matt fidgets, eager to get moving. "I *know*."

"I didn't see you here."

Matt doesn't wait for a second invitation. He pivots away from Francesca and makes a beeline for the comms cupboard.

Around a couple more corners in a quieter part of the school, Matt looks over his shoulder. With the coast still clear, he yanks the heavy door open and disappears inside to a whirr of blinking lights and security cameras showing footage of various angles of the school. Grabbing the keyboard in front of the computer monitor, Matt's fingers scurry over the keys as he finds the backdoor into the system and types in his commands. It'll give him five minutes before chaos is unleashed.

Mission accomplished, Matt darts out of the cupboard and finds the halls now filled with students. Cursing the human obstacles, he weaves a path around the growing hoards and heads for the gym. He pushes his way along the last hall against the overflow of excitement. Finally. Panting, he pulls the door wide. Silver is in the middle of the training mats, her shoulders hunched, her fists clenched. She turns as light spills into the gym from the open door, and her silver eyes focus on his. Matt gives her a nod, silently telling her it's time to go. All those plans they hatched after Diana's death… well, it's time.

"Let's go," Matt says, waving her over.

Kyle follows her as she starts toward him, puts a hand on her shoulder. "You don't have to go. Just wait. They can't do this. You'll see." Oh, Kyle. They talked about this. His head is still in the clouds, unwilling to admit his world is about to come crashing down. He is an eternal optimist. Can't believe the nanite he took last year is all going to go to waste. Except it won't when he joins them in the hideout. They need abilities like his.

Without warming, Silver doubles over. Concern has Matt taking a few steps into the gym as she puts a hand on the floor and struggles to stay upright.

"Silver?" Matt questions. Is she having a panic attack? They don't have time for a panic attack.

Silver pants for air, regains her feet, musters a smile.

"Dude, what happened?" Kyle asks her.

"Just a panic attack," Silver says, still breathless. "I get them sometimes."

Ever since her mother was thrown in prison.

With the countdown ticking in his head, Matt grabs her hand and tugs her out of the doors. She follows him as they run into the hall.

"Where are we going?" she yells over the jostling kids as she tightens her grip on his hand. Students are everywhere. Some whooping and flying around, others trying to get through the metal detectors and outside. No one is getting anywhere fast.

"Away from here," Matt calls over his shoulder.

They weave through a group of bulks high-fiving over their heads, under a group of fairies with butterfly wings skimming the ceiling, and straight into a frightened unadjusted on a mission to get up close and personal with the exit.

"Watch it!" the student growls.

Silver yanks on Matt's hand. "Wait! My cuff. I'm never going to make it through the doors without setting the alarms off."

Matt nudges her side, suppressing a cocky grin. "Don't worry about that."

The unadjusted kid who growled a warning at them makes his move for the front doors, but a security guard tasers him until he's left convulsing on the floor, other alts stepping over his head. Some of them stepping *on*.

A few seconds later, as they push past a group of band kids with more fingers than necessary, the fire alarms wail and sprinklers rain down on them. *Perfect timing*.

"Did you do that?" Silver smiles at him, a smile that lights up his insides.

Already soaked, Matt grins. "Come on!" He pulls her toward the fire exit. Together, they dart through the emergency doors.

Outside, they dash around the corner to the back of the building. Avoiding the side entrances, they hurry for the chain-link fence at the end of the football field. A swirl of summer rain clouds scud across the sky. Army drones buzz all over the city's roofs. Shaped like mosquitos, their elongated noses carry a revolving camera. Thankfully, they're not pointed in their direction—for now. Matt returns his focus to his feet, increasing his pace, but Silver is already a blur up ahead.

"Silver, wait up! You're running really fast!"

"Isn't that the point?" She pumps her legs until she reaches the fence.

"I can't keep up with you," Matt calls as he tries to close the distance between them. Nope. Too much screen time.

She waits at the top of the fence. They clamber over it and drop to the dirt path below.

"You okay?" Matt tilts his head to look at Silver and nudges her foot with his. There isn't a drop of sweat on her, but they are both soaked through from the sprinklers. "You been running marathons I didn't know about?"

Silver shrugs. "Must be those protein drinks. And I've been training in the gym with Claus."

"I wish you'd done some training for me too."

Silver laughs. "I told you racing speedsters in a computer game wasn't going to make you fast."

"Yeah, well, it was worth a try."

"Come on, we need to keep moving."

They take off down the street. Around the corner, heading toward the city, sprinting down familiar roads. Past Mo's ice cream parlor where Matt always orders mint choc chip with a flake. Past the deli his mom likes to buy cold cuts from. And the dance shop where Lyla gets all her gear. His heart gives a tight squeeze. *Lyla. Megan.* Where are they now?

Familiarity falls away quicker than a black hole swallowing a star. Despite the plans he's been making for the last two years, despite knowing everything a resistance movement could unleash, Matt never expected *this*. As they run into a war zone, the reality of the situation slams into him.

Altereds sprint/fly/charge/ along sidewalks and roads, shouting and whistling at each other, pointing out unadjusteds who crouch behind parked cars or hide in the back of shops. The unsuspecting unadjusteds try to run. A couple are caught and cuffed. A couple more are thrown to the ground. Another is shot. A bullet through the head. No nanite pill for him.

A shop window implodes, scattering glass for yards, sending shrapnel into a group of fairies, tearing their wings apart. Their murderous eyes scan the street, whisk over Matt and Silver, before they charge into the shop, yelling for justice.

Bulks and ogres in National Guard uniform carrying machine guns march down the middle of the street, yelling at anyone in their way. A tank rolls by, its caterpillar wheels crushing trash left in the gutters. A girl with swan wings flies by over their heads in the no-fly zone. Matt spins a quick circle, scanning for an exit. Or any place that isn't filled to the brim with alts. They are everywhere. Nowhere is safe. During all the planning, the timing was supposed to be theirs. But President Bear hit the button way before anyone was expecting it. And now...this.

Matt jostles from foot to foot. "Shit, Silver. Where do we go?"

Silver glances at her flashing ankle cuff. A tremor of fears slices through him. They need to get it off. Or they're both dead.

Another shop window shatters. Then a report of rapid gunfire pierces the chaos. Followed by agonized screams. Matt and Silver instinctively duck, breathing hard, scanning their surroundings.

"You have to run, Matt." Silver stills, locks her beautiful eyes on him. "The guards will be after me."

Matt's chest seizes and he can't suck in a breath. There is no way he is leaving her out here with an enormous neon sign highlighting her location. Nope. No. *No fucking way.* "I am *not* leaving you."

Matt takes her hand, notes it's as clammy as his own, and pushes her around a corner into a deserted alley. A couple of dumpsters spill their contents into oily puddles. A stray dog limps by on three legs. It also has three eyes.

Matt kneels at Silver's feet, the rough cement lacerating his knees, unable to look away from the blinking red light on the cuff. How the hell is he supposed to get it off? But he has to think of something, or they're both goners. Knowing he doesn't have the right tools with him, he fiddles with the buttons anyway. His heart kicks against his ribs, refusing to believe they will be caught so quickly. The resistance is relying on him. And they need Silver's father.

His hands shake, but he can't give into the fear. *Shut it down.* This is what he planned for. What he prepared for. He's practiced for these scenarios, knows how to regain his focus when the shit is hitting the fan. But no one told him what it was going to feel like to lose Silver. He has no room for fear, so he shuts it down. Steadying himself, Matt takes a breath. He can do this. He digs deep for his courage. Finds it. At least, more than he had a minute ago, and uses it to steady his hands and pause his cycling thoughts.

"If only I had something sharp," he says as the cuff releases a high-pitched electronic whine.

"You mean like this?" Silver plants a badass throwing knife in front of his face.

Matt raises both brows and releases a low whistle. "Exactly. Where did you get a think like that?"

"Claus."

Matt tuts approvingly, takes the knife, and sets to work on the cuff. Now that he has the tip of the blade to apply the right pressure in the right place, he can set her free. Hope unfurls its wings in his chest.

Her legs twitch all over the place as Matt attempts to concentrate. "Hold still, Silver."

"I'm trying. Can't you get it off?"

An announcement blares over a loudspeaker. "All people are to remain inside. Your nanite representative will be with you in due course."

Soldiers march by, pointing their weapons at fearful faces. "Stay inside! Do not make me use this on you!"

Matt glances up at his best friend, a grimace on his face. "This is going to hurt a bit."

"Hurt? Why does it need to hurt? Haven't you been working on this stuff in that weapons and robotics class?"

Matt suppresses a smile. "It has an anti-tamper shock dispenser."

"Anti-tamper..." An electric current zaps her ankle and she flinches.

"Ouch." Matt shakes his hand, then sticks his thumb and forefinger in his mouth. He hands the knife back.

The ankle cuff clatters to the tarmac, its red light flashing manically. Matt stomps on it until the light dims and dies.

"Cell phone?"

Silver shakes her head. "Left it at school."

He removes his own from his back pocket, chucks it on the ground, and stomps on that too.

Matt grabs Silver's hand and eyes the mouth of the alley. "Let's put a little distance between us and that cuff."

They take off again at a fast walk to avoid raising suspicion, keeping to what little shadows the mid-morning sun offers. They stick to the back alleys, climbing over dumpsters and slipping down high walls. Matt curses his lack of exercise as he leads her toward the park, which stands between them and her home. Now that Silver is safe, they need her father. Everything depends on him. When they skirt into the street, a bulk points at them. He shouts, but a commotion in a shop at his rear draws his attention away.

A few minutes later, they reach the park, but soldiers march through the grassy lawns here too. Matt pulls Silver under the cascading fronds of a weeping willow, the scent of grass and soil surrounding them. Nature. Natural things.

"We need a plan," Silver says, shifting her weight from one foot to the other. "I can't run all the way to my cousin's like this."

Matt dips his head as guilt curls in his stomach. There is so much he hasn't told her, to keep her safe. But apparently she has been keeping secrets too. "Your cousin's?"

Her words come out in one long rush as she toys with the hem of her shorts. "I was going to escape. My second cousin has a hunting lodge upstate. Thought I'd just get there and think about how to get my mom out." She smooths a loose strand of hair away from her face and sets her jaw. "But I need to go back for my dad first."

A smile blooms on Matt's lips. He may have been unable to tell her of his plans, but they think alike. Of course she has made plans of her own.

"There *is* a plan," Matt says. "But it doesn't involve your cousin."

Silver looks left and right, then steps closer, a cute little frown on her face. "A plan for what?"

"For the unadjusteds to escape the classist rule of the alts."

She blanches, her mouth gaping open, looks him up and down. And dammit, he knows he's impressed her.

"How?" she asks.

"People have been talking about leaving the city for a while now, in case something like this happened." His jaw hardens as he surveys the park through the weeping branches. "We found a cave system where we can hide until we figure out what to do. We've been running supplies there for a few months now. But with this announcement coming sooner than we thought, everything's gone to hell. It's a mess. We aren't ready—"

"Your family? You're all involved?"

Matt shakes his head. "Just me. And hundreds of others. Because of you. And because of my family. Megan's just turned twelve. She can't be forced to take a nanite."

She is one of the reasons he joined the resistance. She made him see things he was blind to. She doesn't have to be in a chair. She could take a regeneration nanite to regain the use of her legs. Plenty of people in the same situation have. And she's twelve now, she's reached the age limit. There's nothing to worry about it. But she spent a long afternoon telling him she had no intention of taking a nanite. That the chair was part of her, but it didn't define her. That the experience made her the person she is, and she doesn't want to mess with that. He's not sure when she got so wise. But what will happen to her now? What if she's forced to take a wing nanite? To be able to fly but unable to use her legs? It's ridiculous, and Matt has no idea what she may be forced to ingest.

"Where is this cave?" Silver asks, her hands curling into the fabric of his T-shirt.

"Though the forest."

She blows her cheeks out. "Our forest?"

Matt nods.

"Matt, there are wolves in that forest now. Altered wolves." Her hands fly to her cheeks as if trying to prevent the color leaching from them.

"I know. But we don't have a choice." Matt narrows his eyes. "You heard what President Bear says. Failure to comply will result in *unfortunate circumstances.*"

"My mother," Silver whispers. Matt clenches his fist. He knew Dr. Margaret Melody would be Silver's one hesitation.

The one thing that might keep her here, unable to run. "Or worse."

Silver peers through the branches of the willow. Everything remains quiet. When she turns back to face him, her eyes glisten. He is asking so much of her. To desert her own mother. Matt's not sure he could do that. But she and her father have no future if they don't run. And the unadjusteds will have no future either.

"How do we get there?"

"Enter at the north end." Matt finds the confidence that deserted him during their sprint through the city. This is what he is good at. "It's a three-day hike to the ruined village, then another three days directly southeast. You remember how to use a compass?"

"Yes, of course." She rolls her eyes and that makes him laugh.

"And you remember how to be a little bit violent?"

She grins. "You bring the smarts, I'll bring the muscle."

They high-five, then wince as the sound carries through the branches.

Silver starts pacing from one end of the enclosed space to the other, opening her mouth several ties to speak, only to snap it shut again. They are running out of time, but Matt doesn't have the heart to hurry her. This is new. He just gave her a grenade with the pin pulled. She needs a few. And he needs to implant this image of her in his brain before they go their separate ways.

Abruptly, she stops pacing and walks up to him, getting up in his space, leaving barely a gap between them. Her eyes turn accusatory. "Why didn't you tell me about this?"

Matt grabs her hand, picks a leaf off her sweatshirt. "I didn't want to put you in danger. With your mother in prison..."

The branches and leaves sway in a breeze, bringing the acrid stench of gunpowder. How many unadjusteds will be killed today? And not just today, but in the coming weeks when they refuse to comply. Matt and the rest of the resistance leaders have done their best to spread the word throughout Central City and beyond, but there are only so many risks they can take without endangering themselves.

Silver plants her arms over her chest. "Were you going to leave without me?"

Matt's head snaps up, shock coating him in an uncomfortably thick layer. He uncrosses her arms and pins her wrists to her sides. "Never," he says, and means it. "But I can't go with you now. I need to go back for my family. They don't know what I'm involved in...I need to get them to safety."

Silver dips her head. "So I'll meet you there?"

Matt moves his hand to her chin, lifts it, locks his eyes on her and puts all his love into that gaze. For several heartbeats they stare at each other. "Yes." It is as simple as that. A few days and they will be together again. Matt shuts out the invading thoughts of danger.

Silver's shoulders drop and she sags against him. He guides her to the trunk of the tree where they huddle together as soldiers make the occasional sweep through the park. He hugs her, his arms tight around her waist, afraid to let go. Because then everything will begin. Taking advantage of their tight hug, he presses his nose into her hair, inhaling her citrusy scent, committing it to memory. As well as the feel of his arms around her. He can't bear to let go.

Silver rests her forehead against his. "I need to get to my dad."

"I know." Matt sighs. "But before you go, I have something for you." He digs into his pocket and removes a small, wrapped box, the paper pink with flying fairies. "I thought you'd enjoy the irony."

"I don't think there's a cheerleading team in the country that doesn't have fairy wings now."

"Overgrown, dress-up butterfly wings."

Silver touches the small package as if it might contain the Holy Grail. Or a bomb.

"Open it," Matt whispers.

Finally, she tears open the paper, ripping across a fairy's face. Inside is a black jewelry box. Matt holds his breath. He spent hours picking it out. As Silver lifts the lid, she gasps and her eyes fill. Matt's chest swells with emotions he doesn't know how to contain. Silver plucks the necklace from the box. The pendant is a single musical note, a quaver.

"On account of your last name, Melody," Matt says. "And your love of guitar."

"It's beautiful, Matt. Thank you." Her hand floats forward and rests on his chest. Can she feel his heart pounding under her touch? "This is the nicest present anyone's ever given me."

"You're welcome." Matt kisses her lightly on the top of her head, not daring anything more. This isn't the time for that. But he wants to. He wants to wrap his arms around her and tell her how much he loves her. He wants to kiss her, to touch her, to make love to her. But his feelings are his own, and now isn't the time for confessions.

Instead, with shaking hands, he plucks the necklace from her palm and moves behind her. She lifts her hair for him and he fastens the clasp at her nape, his fingers brushing against her warm skin. How he'd love to press his lips there too.

When he faces her once more, the pendant hangs below her collarbone, catching a reflected ray of light.

"And now we need to go." Stealing himself for the imminent separation, Matt grabs her hands and soaks up all the things that make her her in that one touch. "I'll see you at the cave, right?"

"Yes."

"With your dad?" He presses his thumbs into her palms, attempting to portray how important it is that she brings her father.

"I promise." She wraps her hands around his thumbs and squeezes.

Matt forces a smile onto his lips, but he can feel the tension in it. He takes a step backward, still hanging onto her hand. "I'll see you in a few days. A week, max."

And then he dashes out from the cover of the tree, not looking back, because then he would never leave.

CHAPTER 3

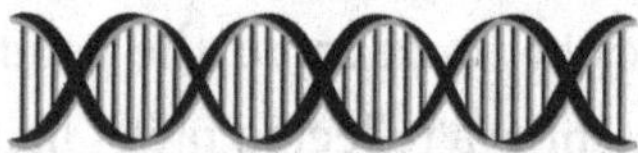

MATT BURSTS through the front door of his home, shouting before he shuts the door behind him. "Let's go! Grab the go bags! Nanite reps are everywhere. Hustle, let's hustle!"

His parents look up from the kitchen table as he marches down the hall. Einstein barks. He glances at the cake on the counter, completed, the perfect shade of pink. There is no way he can bring it with them. Silver will have to go without a cake this year. Again.

"Go bags?" his mom asks.

His dad frowns. "Go where?"

He scans their faces, at the tension hardening their features. There is so much he has to tell them, but there is no time.

"Do you trust me?" he asks.

They both nod. Megan claps.

"We don't want to take any nanites, do we?"

Silently, they all shake their heads.

"I don't have time to tell you everything," he says as he pulls bags from the hall cupboard that no one uses. "There is a resistance movement. There's a hideout. And we're going. Now. Where's Lyla?"

"At her audition," his mom replies.

Matt releases a tight breath. "She hasn't come home?"

His dad shakes his head. "It's only been forty-five minutes since the announcement." *Is that all?* "They might be keeping her there. We haven't been able to get through. Cell networks are jammed."

Megan glances at her own cell. "She's still there. According to the location app."

"We'll pick her up on the way." Matt swings back into action, carrying the bags to the car. He hopes he's thought of everything because he doesn't have time to double check things now. Megan's off-road wheels are already in the back of the car. Food and water and other essentials have been delivered to the cave, but it won't be enough. Depending on how many people turn up.

"Where are we going?" his mom asks as she follows him out to the car, her feet in a sensible pair of sneakers. His T-shirt is still damp from the sprinklers, but he doesn't have time to change it now.

Their gazes lock as Matt loads the car. He notes the tension in her face, the way she's rubbing her temple like she's got one of her migraines, but there isn't time to ease her into this. "We're going to be hiking. I've got clothes, tents, sleeping bags, toothbrushes..." he trails off, he doesn't have time for this. "I've got everything covered. Just get in the car."

With a quick nod, his mom slides into the front passage seat. As he goes back for more bags, Matt spots several neighbors doing the same as him. Loading up. Getting out. A few of them will be going to the cave. He gives them a silent nod of acknowledgement.

His dad wheels Megan out of the house, with Einstein padding beside her. Matt picks up his dog and loads him into the trunk with the bags, and his dad settles Megan in the back seat and folds the wheelchair. They are packed. They are ready. It is time to leave.

A brick of tension grows in Matt's stomach as he hesitates. Everything is about to change. There is no coming back from this. If they run, they will always be running. He doubts then. Would taking a nanite be so bad? He looks at his family. Regeneration for Megan. Maybe wings for his mother. His dad would suit speed. But they are all expensive. The government will make them pay for the nanites and Matt's family can't afford those. They'll be stuck with something from the backlog pile, the discount bucket, something likely dangerous. And he won't allow any of his family to foam out at the change.

Checking his resolve, he slides into the back seat beside Megan as his dad starts the engine.

"I'm scared," Megan says.

Her face is tight, her skin pale, her eyes haunted. She's too young for this.

Matt gives her hand a gentle squeeze. "Everything is going to be okay. I'd never let anything happen to you. Your big brother is on the case." He holds out his knuckles for a punch and she obliges, a fragile smile creeping onto her lips.

Matt sits up and clenches the back of the driver's seat. "We need to get Lyla and then we need to get out of here."

As his dad takes a corner at speed, narrowly avoiding an alt with antlers charging down the middle of the street, Matt relays the instructions about the secret parking spot he set up at the entrance to the forest.

His mom raises her eyebrows at him in the rearview. "How long have you been planning this?"

"Two years," Matt replies.

"Since Margaret...?"

"Yep." And that is the only reply needed. Silver's mother and his are best friends. Grew up together. They spent weekends and vacations and lazy Sunday afternoons together. They are the best memories Matt has. But it all stopped two years ago when Margaret was found guilty of treason and the remaining Melodys were no longer allowed out of their apartment complex.

Matt swivels in his seat as a loud screech of clashing metal sounds behind them. A collision. Hoods steaming, drivers okay but getting out. Both alts. Both yelling at each other. One with a narwhal spike protruding from his head stabs the other through the chest. No warning. Pins him against the steaming vehicle. Dead. Just like that. What the...?

Matt's stomach clenches as he turns back around. Did he just witness a murder? But why are alts killing each other? Surely this is what they want?

Several altereds run in the streets. Matt catches sight of a blurry speedster. A woman teleporting. A toddler breathing fire. *Jesus H.* They are running and fighting, all going at each other with whatever weapons they can lay their hands on. A trash can lid, a hammer, a hubcap. Matt cradles his sister to his chest and puts a hand over her eyes.

"What's going on?" Megan asks, allowing him to blind her view.

"Nothing you need to see."

His Dad's face is paler than bone. His mom tucks her chin to her chest and squeezes her eyes shut. His dad swerves as an altered with hedgehog prickles running the length of his spine holds a baseball bat aloft. As he brings it down to strike a woman with blue skin, she teleports out of danger. A female teenager with butterfly wings and antennae growing out of her head thrusts a knife into the stomach of a male teen with a mouth where his abdomen is supposed to be.

"What the hell is going on?" His dad grips tight to the steering wheel and lives out all his racing car dreams. If he ever had any.

Matt shakes his head. "I don't know."

"Just how many people are part of this resistance?" his mom asks.

"Hundreds. Thousands across the country," Matt says. "But this? This isn't the resistance. This is—"

"Carnage," his dad says.

"I think it's the God factor," Matt says.

"The *what?*" his mom asks.

"Something Rufus and Margaret used to talk about," Matt says as his dad takes another corner at speed. "Back when they were allowed to talk. I remember them saying there were weird results during the nanite trials. Something they couldn't explain. Something about ingesting too much animal DNA, that it could change you, permanently. That you needed to be around an unadjusted to keep you sane. They called it the God Factor."

An altered male with a rhino horn sprouting from each shoulder rolls across the front of the car, then slams his horns into the chest of a female with scaled skin. His dad slows to avoid the alts warring in the streets.

"And now the unadjusteds are running, there's no one left to keep them sane. Is that possible?" his mom asks. "So quickly?"

"When we see them again, we'll ask," his dad says. "In the meantime, we need to get the hell out of Dodge."

"Maybe they'll all kill each other," Matt says. But he doesn't want all the alts to die. It's not just the unadjusteds who are unhappy with the nanite program. Plenty of alts have their own personal axes to grind, for various reasons, and they make up a significant part of the resistance. They need them. They need each other.

"Bear will have something up his sleeve," his dad says. "He may be a tyrant, but he's an intelligent tyrant."

They round a corner near the dance studio to find the far end of the road filled with soldiers heading away from them. Skyscrapers cast foreboding shadows over the car. They are going in the opposite direction of the forest, but they can't leave without his sister. His Dad pulls to a stop on the side of the road. The tension in Matt's body rachets up a few notches. A nausea in his stomach, a vice at the back of his neck, an ache in his limbs.

"This is impossible," his dad says. "We'll never get through."

"Stay here." Matt unbuckles his seatbelt. "I'll get Lyla."

His mom lurches in her seat and grabs his arm. "Wait—"

"It's only two blocks."

"But the altereds," his mom says.

"Bet you're wishing you got me a speed nanite right about now, huh?" Matt attempts to lighten the mood.

His mom pins him with one of her looks. "That is *not* funny."

His dad catches his eye in the rearview. "Go. Grab her, and let's get out of here."

Matt holds his gaze for a couple seconds. So much passes between them, nothing either can put into words.

"Be careful!" his mom calls as he throws the car door open.

Matt runs along the sidewalk, pumping his arms, scanning the street ahead for soldiers or alts. He skirts around a winged altered shoving a knife into the side of an alt with antlers. Antler guy turns, stabs the winged alt with his horns, piercing an eye. Blood stains the tarmac. Matt runs by. No time to process the horror of that now.

A few seconds later, the dance studio looms into view. Matt dashes through the doors and into the reception area. A swivel chair is overturned and digital display posters are cracked and shattered. Once of them continues to play a show reel from the studio's most recent recital. Sound off. On the screen, Lyla turns a perfect pirouette.

"Lyla?" Matt calls. "Are you here?"

Matt runs into the main studio. It is deserted. Not even a

dust bunny hiding in a corner. Shouts from outside permeate the windows. The mirrors lining the far wall are cracked, one of them shattered, its jagged pieces threatening to spill into the room. A grand piano in the corner slopes dangerously, one of its legs chopped off at the knee. He ventures further into the room.

"Lyla?" Matt hisses her name, afraid of drawing attention from outside. "Are you here?"

A small noise snags his attention. Tense, he creeps around the edge of the piano, feet crunching over broken glass, and finds a young girl with pink butterfly wings. She can't be much older than Megan. Tear tracks stain her cheeks and her unraveled hair falls over her face.

Matt crouches in front of her, careful to avoid planting his hand into a pile of glass. "Hey. What's your name?"

She looks up at him with bright, trusting eyes. "Sofia."

"Where is everyone?" he asks, giving the deserted room another cursory glance. He spots Lyla's phone under the piano. The protective case showing a picture of a ballerina slipper is stained and cracked. Just like the phone itself. "I thought there was an audition today?"

Sofia's eyes widen as sirens sound in the distance. Pop shots follow, and they both hold their breath.

"The nanite reps came in the middle of it." Sofia wipes her cheek, only to smudge a streak of dust across it.

"What happened?" Matt's heart pounds way too hard. "Where did everyone go?"

"Some of them got away." Sofia cocks her shoulder. "Others were taken by the soldiers. They left me alone." She flutters a wing.

She's already an alt. Maybe got her wings for her twelfth or thirteen birthday.

"What about Lyla?" Matt asks, trying not to shake the terrified girl. "Do you know Lyla? Lyla Lawson?"

"I think they took her." Sofia's wings fold into her back. "She fought. They hit her on the head and dragged her out."

Shit. Fear burns its way up Matt's throat. "Do you know where they took them?"

"I'm not sure." Sofia looks at her slippered feet, plays with her covered toes. "I heard something about a compound. Somewhere they can be assessed."

Without warning, one of the mirrors in the frames shatters and hundreds of tiny pieces of glass cascade to the floor. Sofia screams. Matt cradles her to his chest.

"We can't stay here." The noise will draw attention.

"I'm scared." Sofia's entire body trembles in his arms.

"Where are you parents?" Matt asks. He doesn't have time to reunite her with them, but maybe they're on their way here now.

"In the city. They're both unadjusted. They used all their money to get me my wings..." a sob strangles her voice.

"We don't have time to find them right now," Matt says the words as gently as he can.

Sofia coughs and wipes her eyes. "I know."

Matt stands, then helps the girl to her feet. "My family is parked down the street. Come with us. We're going to a safe place."

He won't leave her here. Even if she is clearly an alt and of no interest to the nanite reps. He won't leave a kid the age of his sister to fend for herself. Not with murderous rampages going on outside the studio. In all the streets of Central City. Although he's prepared to hoist her over his shoulder and drag her to safety, he'd prefer it if she came quietly.

Sofia folds her hand in his and follows him out of the studio.

CHAPTER 4

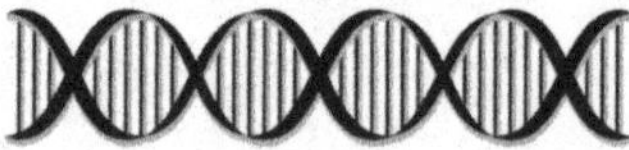

MATT CHECKS the street before he makes a move. Tugging Sofia's hand, they step onto the sidewalk. When he is sure the coast is clear, he urges her into a run. Her wings flutter and she launches herself into the air, flying along beside him.

They both duck as bullets sound. After a few seconds, when Matt realizes he hasn't been hit, he pulls Sofia's small body in front of his and thrusts her forward. He doesn't dare glance over his shoulder as he pushes all his speed and adrenaline into his legs, ignoring the way his lungs seize and his heart pounds.

The family car appears. Matt lunges for it, yanking open the door and pushing Sofia inside, jumping in after her.

A bullet hits the back window, shattering it. Megan and Sofia scream. Einstein barks from the footwell.

"Go, go, go!" Matt yells, covering his head with his arms.

The car tears away, his dad hunched in the seat, swerving down the road. Matt spares a look through the shattered back windscreen, spots a sight that fills him with dread.

"Get down!" Matt yells. "Everyone, get down!" He pulls Sofia and Megan under the cover of the seats, shields them with his own body as a bulk soldier takes aim. Bullets slam into the back of the car.

The car fishtails, both his parents yelling and screaming. Then the tires find purchase and the car speeds through the streets. Matt risks another glance out the window to see they are now alone. He takes a moment to buckle his seatbelt, then sags against the seat. *Jesus fucking Christ.*

"Where's Lyla?" his dad asks when things are quieter and they've all caught their breath.

"She wasn't there," Matt says, giving Megan and Sofia a quick once-over to make sure they aren't injured. "Sofia says they were taken to a compound for assessment."

Sofia curls into Megan, and his sister wraps her arms around the butterfly girl. He's proud of her. Putting her own fear aside to comfort another. He hopes someone is doing the same for Lyla. It's what he should be doing for Silver.

"What kind of compound?" His mom turns in her seat. "Sofia?"

Sofia shakes her head, tries to speak, but her words come out strangled and croaky.

"We have to find her," Megan says.

"We can't go back now," his mom says. "It's too danger-ous. We could all be caught...or worse..."

The seriousness of her words settles around Matt. This is no joke. People are dying. Both unadjusteds and altereds. Even though he knew a day like this would come, even though he's been planning for it...he can't shake the horror he's witnessed in the last two hours. It's going to haunt his dreams. But he can't let it invade his thoughts. Not now. He has to keep functioning. *Shut it down.*

Megan twists beside him, clawing for the door. "We can't leave her behind!"

Matt grabs her wrist and holds it until she calms. "We don't have a choice."

"We need to get to safety," his dad says. "Take stock. Then we'll figure out where they've taken Lyla."

A heavy silence fills the car as his dad follows Matt's directions down a narrow track and into the forest. A knot of tension releases. Finally, they are safe. *Safer.* There is still a six-day hike to complete, with a twelve-year-old in a wheelchair, modified wolves, and God knows what else.

A half hour later, Matt instructs his father down a series of tight turns that the car is almost too wide for, but then a small clearing opens up in front of them and the vehicle comes to a stop. They all take a minute. Not talking, just staring at the forest beyond the broken windows, taking in the startling silence as the engine cools.

Stealing himself, Matt opens his door and jumps to the ground. He opens the trunk, clears the shattered glass away from the luggage, earning himself a couple of shallow nicks on his palms, and starts loading their bags into a pile. His parents come outside to help. Megan and Sofia stay inside.

His dad removes Megan's wheelchair, looks at the slender wheels, then the rough forest terrain.

"Off-road tires are in the back," Matt says, and his dad gets to work changing the tires.

Einstein hovers by Matt, sniffing the bags, scenting the

food packed for him. Matt gives him a scrunch behind the ears and the dog leans into his touch, then licks his hand. When Megan's wheelchair is ready to go, Matt lifts her out of the car and into the chair.

"Where are we going?" Megan asks, craning her neck to look down the dirt track they came along.

"On an adventure," Matt replies, keeping his voice light.

His mom stands by his side, her face raised to the tree canopy, scattered sunlight dancing over her skin. She looks... peaceful. Which saddens Matt, because it's not going to last. There is so much ahead of them. Obstacles he hasn't had time to prepare them for.

Sofia edges out of the car, her entire body trembling. Adrenaline. Shock. Trauma. They're all going to feel it. But they have to keep it together.

Matt picks up the bag he packed for Lyla. The clothes will be too big for Sofia, but it's all they have. "Think you can carry this bag?" he asks the young girl.

She nods and Matt slips the straps onto her shoulders, careful not to damage her wings. Megan's bag is slung from the handles of her wheelchair. The rest of them shrug into their own packs. Before Matt slips his on, he covers the car with branches he cut down a few weeks ago, concealing most of it from view. They shouldn't have been followed into the woods, but in case anyone happens along the trail, he doesn't want to give them a reason to go looking for them.

"Where are we going?" his dad asks.

"Three days to the ruined village," Matt replies. It's a place they all know. The location of a couple of their camping spots over the years. But the family hasn't been there in months. Too many wolves. Modified wolves. Too deep into the forest. "And then onto the cave."

They start walking, his dad pushing Megan. His Mom with an arm around Sofia.

"How long...how long have you been involved in this?" his mom asks, a new look in her eyes. Here, in the woods, he is the one giving instructions. Was it only this morning they were discussing the color of icing?

"How big is this...resistance?" his dad asks.

They barrel questions at him. So many questions. He doesn't have the energy to answer, but they deserve to know. So he tells them. Everything. How from the moment Silver's mother was arrested, he knew something like this would happen. It started with his teacher, Mrs. Montoya —Francesca—catching him in a whispered conversation with Kyle about the altereds. Kyle can't keep his mouth shut—way too much energy and excitement—and the way she looked at them both told Matt she felt the same. She had friends. Adult friends who were forming groups. Before a week had passed, he and Kyle were fully entrenched. With Kyle's speed, they scouted several potential locations in only a few weeks before they settled on the cave. Then they started driving in supplies. Matt's primary thought had been food, water, and first aid supplies. The journey to the cave would be treacherous for many. His family could come across any number of obstacles. So, the first aid supplies. A doctor would be better.

While several adults in the resistance were tasked with kitting out the cave, a few who had access to certain materials brought them to Matt so he could construct his plan for a defensive perimeter. A series of connected voice activated bombs that he planned to bury around the cave entrance. They were in his bag now. Far more important than clean underwear. Although he might come to regret that decision before too long.

His parents don't say a single word as he speaks, but their mouths gape wider with each sentence he utters.

"So all that time you were at your robotics and tech club, you were really forming a resistance?" his mom asks, maneuvering around a dense clump of ferns.

Matt grins. "I went to the club too."

"What about Silver?" his dad asks. "Rufus?"

Matt nods. "She's going to meet us there. With Rufus. And I'm praying he can help us find a solution to this whole mess."

"You think it's possible?" his dad questions. "A solution to the divide? A solution to the enhancements?"

Matt tilts his head as he navigates over roots and around thick trees. They are deep in the woods, the only sounds... natural—bird song, the rustling of small animals, the buzzing of insects, Einstein's gentle barks, and he considers the questions. He has hope. Which can be a dangerous thing. He has no idea what's possible. But there is no going back.

"I don't know what the future looks like," Matt says slowly, choosing his words carefully so as not to upset his sister or Sofia. "But we can't go back home. I don't know for how long. And I'm hoping like hell Rufus can help us find a way out of this mess. If anyone can, it's him."

His parents both take in his words with grim acceptance. Matt removes a machete from the side of his pack and hacks at the thickening undergrowth so his dad can push Megan a little easier. They are all already sweating.

His mom walks close to him, out of earshot of the others. "What about Lyla? How will we find out where they've taken her? How will we get her back?"

Matt's stomach clenches as he considers. Lyla not being with them was not something he prepared for. They didn't know of the compounds. Many families will be separated. And they won't sit around and do nothing, let their loved ones be imprisoned...mistreated...experimented on...Hell, there is no way he isn't going after Lyla. But only after he gets his family to safety.

But then there are his responsibilities in the cave. He and Francesca and Claus are the resistance leaders. People will look to them. He can't desert them. Not when he is needed.

He looks at his family. They are together. They will help him. "I don't know yet," Matt admits. "I don't know what these compounds are, where they are, how secure they are, what they'll do to her..." Desperation claws up his throat and his breath catches.

His mom puts a hand on his shoulder. Although her features are tight, her voice is kind. "It's okay, Matt. We'll find her. And I'm so fucking proud of you."

He raises a brow at the curse. She never curses. She lets out a laugh and the sound eases a little of the tension coiled so tightly inside him.

"I love you too," he says, winding an arm around her

waist. They walk that way for a few paces until their heavy bags get in the way and they are forced to separate.

A couple of hours later, they stop for a break. They are all drenched in sweat. There is a puddle of it in the small of Matt's back and in places he'd rather not share. While his mom stretches Megan out on the ground and massages her legs, Einstein licking her face, Matt digs through the bags for the packet food. Most of them are a variety of noodles. All you have to do is open the package and a chemical reaction takes place, warming the cooked food to a favorable temperature. They get one each. Matt wolf's his down while the others eat and sets about filling their water canisters. When he planned the route, he was careful to keep their path near to the stream. Summer in the city and forest always brings high temperatures and high humidity. Thank God there is an underwater lake in the cave with an endless supply of fresh water. It's one of the reasons they picked the location.

"I like it here," Megan says, staring dreamily at the sky.

Sofia lies down beside her. "Me too. It's where butterflies are supposed to live."

Megan turns her head to look at her. "I like your wings."

"I like your wheels."

They smile at each other and a pang of emotion shoots through Matt's chest as Einstein sniffs at the water flasks he's lined up. Although he's tired from the hike, from the run through the city this morning, he can't stop moving. Because then his brain will fill with morbid thoughts and he needs to distract himself from what they've done to Lyla and where Silver is. Has she made it out of the city? Did she convince her dad to run? Are they being tailed? Are they safe?

Matt grits his teeth as a fine tremor runs down his spine. Feeling eyes on him, he snaps his head up as a howl echoes through the forest. Einstein barks. Matt's gaze collides with his dad's. He hurries to Megan and puts her in her chair. But if there is a wolf nearby, one with predatory instincts, they won't be able to run. They will have to fight.

Matt plucks the machete from where it rests on the ground and calls to Einstein to heel. The golden retriever is great at licking faces and fetching a ball, but he's not so great at following instructions. He disappears into the bushes.

"Shit," Matt mutters, taking a few steps to follow the dog, then pulls back as another howl rips through the trees. A different direction. A second wolf. Then a third from behind. A fourth from somewhere off to his left. They are surrounded.

Einstein's barks become fainter, but more insistent. Sofia stands with the bag on her shoulders and her wings folded into her back, her entire slender body trembling.

"Let's go!" Megan calls, waving their parents into action.

They slip into the packs as Matt hands out the flasks. Then he sticks his fingers into his mouth and lets rip a mighty whistle. Einstein barks, comes charging back through the undergrowth, leaves and twigs stuck to his blond coat. Matt strains to listen for other sounds but doesn't hear the wolves. Not for a full five minutes. There is only one howl, moving away.

Einstein sits at Matt's side, wagging his tail, looking up at him as if he deserves a bone. Matt scrunches him behind the ears.

"I think they passed," his mom says.

Or they're circling around.

"They're unlikely to attack a group," his dad says.

Not if they're modified. Or if they're altereds who have taken a wolf nanite. But Matt doesn't voice his thoughts. There's no point freaking everyone out. He holds the machete in a white-knuckle grip and hopes if it comes to it, he'll be able to take on a pack of hungry wolves.

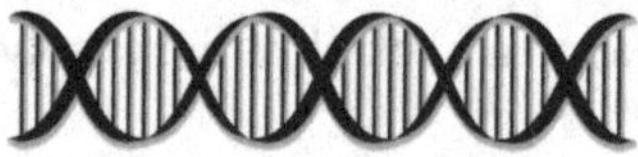

CHAPTER 5

ALERT FOR SOUNDS that don't belong in the forest, Matt leads his family through the thick ferns, hacking at the undergrowth. The trail they were following disappeared an hour ago. They are now in the part of the woods where few humans venture. The wild, uncontained part. Their pace has slowed, their feet tangled in routes, as Matt hacks a path big enough for Megan's chair. But he prepared for this. He planned a path that would be accessible to Megan. Well, as accessible as possible. They follow the stream, which loops around a little more than he likes, but the undergrowth and trees are the tiniest bit thinner next to the water, and so that is the route they must follow.

Sofia is holding up okay. Doesn't say much, only when she's asked a question. Her wings are permanently folded into her back so she doesn't snag the delicate material on whipping branches. His parents give him purposeful looks. They want to talk more but won't risk it in front of his sister and Sofia. Their heads do not need to be filled with President

Bear's atrocities and the fragility of the Lawson family's future. They are too young for this shit. Then again, Megan was too young to be in a car wreck and lose the ability to walk.

He looks at his sister now. A frown sits on her face. Despite what she's been through, she's usually the most optimistic person in the house. Matt doesn't like the frown.

"You okay, squirt?" he asks her.

A one-shoulder shrug is his only response. The frown stays fixed to her face and her gaze is glued to her wheels, the way they bump over roots and pinecones. An uncomfortable tension hangs in the air, mixing with the humidity and insects. Matt scratches at the back of his neck, wishing there was a way he could make Megan feel more comfortable, more...useful. But it is what it is.

Matt hacks at ferns, at low-lying branches, rakes his free hand through his damp hair, slaps insects on his skin. This isn't as fun as he remembers. Now that there are real stakes. With every step, the tension in his chest coils tighter. Silver. He wants to hurry to the cave so they can be reunited, so he can see she is safe, but getting there any faster won't make Silver be there too.

Suddenly, Megan bursts out crying. Matt turns to see she's covered her face with her hands. His mom kneels in front of her. His Dad leans over the chair to look at her. Sofia stands there staring, holding onto the scruff of Einstein's neck.

"What's the matter, sweetheart?" his mom asks, trying to pry one of her hands from her face.

With an exaggerated sigh, Megan drops her hands into

her lap and moves her gaze to each member of her family. "I'm sorry."

Matt frowns. "What for?"

Megan gestures to the chair. "We'd be going a lot faster if it wasn't for me."

"That's not your fault, sweetheart," his mom says, but Matt can hear the tension in her voice.

"Of course it's my fault," Megan says. "I refused to take a regeneration nanite."

Maybe they would go faster if Megan had taken the damn pill. Oh, the irony. To be running away from the very thing that would help her, from the very thing she feels so much guilt over. But then, it's not about taking a pill, it's not about being an altered or an unadjusted. It's about the mind-set. Diana had taken five nanites when she died, and she was the farthest thing from an altered that Matt knew.

Matt crouches in front of his sister, takes in her dirt-streaked face. "Even if you had taken a regeneration nanite, there's no guarantee you wouldn't have experienced side-effects. You could have died."

"He's right," his dad says. "We thought about it for hours. Days. Weeks. And we made a decision with you. Remember, sweetheart?"

"Besides," Matt says. "I remember how slow your running was before the accident."

Megan glares at him, then cracks a hint of a smile.

"We've got this." He holds out his fist for a knuckle punch. Megan taps him back. "We'll get there when we get there. No one is looking for us. These woods cover half the state. It's just going to take some time."

Megan nods, lets out a sigh. "What are we waiting for then?"

They all laugh as his dad resumes pushing the chair. Sofia sticks close to them with a hand on the armrest of the chair, and Einstein doesn't stray far either.

His mom walks in front with Matt, taking a turn with the machete. "That was kind of you."

"It's the truth."

"You've always been good with her."

"She's my sister."

His mom gives him a wry smile. "Not so good with Lyla."

He wants to smile back, hell he wants to give voice to the laugh bubbling up his throat, but he can't, not with Lyla gone. If Lyla was with them, he'd tell his mom it's because she's a brat. But he can't say that now, obviously. "Maybe we're too close in age."

"Maybe."

Darkness hits quick. One minute the scattered sunlight is filtering low through the staggered trees, the next Matt is tripping over roots he can't see. They need to stop for the night. He gestures to a tiny clearing near the edge of the stream. The water should cloak their scent from creatures on the other side. It's too risky to light a fire, so Matt spends an hour building a haphazard den that offers them an illusion of protection. His dad helps him sift leaves and sticks from the ground and roll out the sleeping bags. They eat another packet of food each. Mostly in silence. Occasionally his mom remarks on a type of wildflower growing nearby. His dad talks about how dark it is away from the city. Matt risks the glow of a single flashlight. But now they are all lit up and can't see anything past a few feet into her forest.

After his mom helps Megan to relieve herself and settles her into a sleeping bag, she massages her legs once more. His dad checks her tires. Matt remembered the pump, but he's only got one puncture repair kit, that's all he could fit.

Sofia spots a pink morpho butterfly darting around in the glow of the flashlight. She spreads her wings to show they match, a small smile playing over her lips.

"How long have you had the wings?" Matt asks, craving a hit of sweetness after the salty pasta. He didn't pack anything sweet. There is no room for luxuries. Camping used to be easy, living off the land, eating burned sausages cooked in flames. But it was only ever for a week at a time. He knew he'd get back to his comfortable double bed. Now...now there isn't an end to anything. This is it.

"A little over a year," Sofia says, fluttering the wings gently. "Got them for my twelfth birthday."

"What was it like?" Megan asks as she props herself up on an elbow. "The change? Was it painful?"

Sofia shakes her head. "It tickled. Like a feather floating over my spine."

"That's nice," his mom remarks.

"Do they grow as you grow?" Megan asks.

Sofia nods, allowing her wings to hover a little higher. "Are you all unadjusteds?"

"Yep," Megan says. "All of us."

Matt doesn't bother to correct her. The issues of his enhanced intelligence given to him in vitro is gray at best. He doesn't think of himself as an alt. None of his family does. His mindset is as unadjusted as it gets.

"I'm the only one in my family who is an...altered," Sofia says the word hesitantly. It's not the official word for those who have undertaken genetic enhancement. The official word is 'adjusted.' Hence where 'unadjusted' comes from. But 'altered' is what Matt and Silver have always used. He didn't realize he'd spoken it allowed often enough for Sofia to pick up on. But they aren't the only ones who use it. They went through a phase of calling them the *superfreaks*. But when the resistance started, the members agreed, in light of moving forward in a positive manner and not causing further divide, that the term *superfreak* should be abolished. Matt can see their point, but sometimes, when he comes across an alt with the worst kind of mentality, it is the only appropriate term. "I have two older sisters...my parents...I'm the only one." Her voice hitches at the end.

Matt touches her hand. "They will have been taken to a compound. They'll be safe there."

"I'm not a kid," Sofia says. "I'm not a grown up either, but I know damn well they're not going to do good things to them. It's not a hotel." The vehemence startles Matt. It's the longest sentence she's uttered since she's been with them.

"You're right. I'm sorry." Matt decides revealing the elephant hiding under the bush is the best thing to do. "But I do believe they'll be safe. I happen to know one of the scientists who invented nanites." Sofia's eyes grow wide, wider than the cone of the flashlight. "He has a theory. The altereds. Sorry, the *adjusteds*, can't survive without the unadjusteds. You saw them go nuts in the streets, right?" Sofia nods. "Yeah, well, that' s because they need the unadjusteds. Or those who have only taken one or two nanites. They *need* us. So they're not going to start exterminating us, if that's what everyone is worried about."

None of them know what these compounds are about. It is a plan of Bear's the resistance members have no knowledge of, but he's obviously been preparing for something. He must know about the God factor. He must know altereds can't survive on their own. He must know the unadjusteds are necessary. And so he needed to round them all up and stick them somewhere they can't run, just so the alts can stay sane. Today has proven Rufus' theory is right. And that makes things a hell of a lot more complicated. For everyone.

"Am I going to go insane?" Sofia asks. "I don't want to hurt anyone."

"You've only taken one nanite, right?" Matt asks.

She nods.

"Then you have nothing to worry about."

"Besides, you're with us," Megan says. "We're all unadjusted. We'll keep you sane."

Sofia works her hand into Megan's. Somehow, despite their differences, they are becoming friends. Matt smiles. This has always been his point. It doesn't matter how many pills have been taken. It's about the mindset.

Thoughts of Diana flood his mind. The way the nanites were forced on her by her parents. How she took her fifth and final one...it caused her death. He and Silver were there with her at the end. And of course, now thoughts of Silver invade. Whenever he thinks of her, a physical tension comes along with it. Worry for her safety. Because he loves her so damn much. If anything happens to her...he shakes his head, pushing the thoughts away. *Stay in the present. Stay focused. Don't borrow from tomorrow's problems.*

Claus' advice. Silver is right about him too. He really does speak in fortune cookie.

"We should get some sleep," his mom says. "Dawn comes early in the summer." She helps Sofia into Lyla's sleeping bag.

"Someone should keep watch," Matt says.

Gently, his dad takes the flashlight out of his hand. "I'll take first watch. I'll wake you in a couple hours."

Matt nods, crawls to his sleeping bag, lies down on his stomach. Einstein nestles beside him, the warmth of the dog welcome in the cooling forest. He wraps his arm around him and holds him tight. Einstein gives him one lingering lick across his ear and settles beside him. The rich scent of earth and nature rush up his nose. And Einstein's foul doggie breath. That is his last thought as he falls into a deep and dreamless sleep, in spite of everything.

His eyes flicker open as dawn bruises the sky. It's not a full assault of daylight and he's not sure what woke him, except his entire body is tense. His limbs taut and achy, his chest tight, and a tingle at the back of his neck. Not the good kind. Einstein lies beside him still. Everyone else is asleep. Including his dad, who was supposed to wake him for watch duty.

Matt pushes himself to a sitting position. He surveys the forest, reaches for the machete at his side. Something is wrong.

And then he hears it.

Whop-whop-whop.

The distant churn of helicopter blades flying over the forest. But they can't be looking for him. He's not important enough. They can't know about the resistance already. Most of the members will be heading for the cave, separately. Maybe some have been herded into the compounds. Maybe some of them are dead.

So why the helicopters?

His heart thuds inside his chest, threatening to escape his ribs. *Silver. Rufus. They're on the run.*

At least, he hopes they are. He can't think of another reason the helicopters would be out. Unless it's a news crew reporting on the chaos of the altereds turning murderous. Or there is another high-profile figure on the run. Dammit, it could be any number of things. But he hopes, and kind of not hopes, that it's because of Silver. Because she's out of the city and running. And she can run *fast*. She proved that the other day. Yesterday. Was that only yesterday? He hopes Rufus can keep up with her. Matt has seen him on the treadmill in their apartment countless times. He's in good shape. Maybe he was preparing for escape too.

Matt squeezes his eyes closed as the sound of the rotor blades fade. Einstein curls into his side. Matt flops back onto his sleeping bag but he's too restless to go back to sleep. They should get moving soon anyway. He sits back up, rubs the grit from his eyes, takes a swig of water and swirls it in his mouth before swallowing it down. Offers a bit to Einstein, who laps it up.

Then he rolls to his feet, pretending he has more energy than he feels. Everything aches. From the running, from sleeping on a hard ground. Hopefully, the adrenaline will keep him going. He rolls up his sleeping bag, stuffs it into his pack. The others rouse. Tentative smiles spread through the group. They made it through their first night. Megan and Sofia high-five. Matt smiles at that. He sends a mental high-five in Silver's direction. Diana's too. He doesn't believe in God, in an afterlife, but if there is any part of Diana still hanging around, then she'd be damn proud of him right now.

After they are up and packed, which takes a total of five minutes, Matt helps Megan to her chair and takes a turn pushing her while his dad hacks away with the machete. They eat breakfast on the way—a calorific trail mix combo of nuts and raisins and chocolate. No one complains that they get to eat chocolate for breakfast.

Einstein keeps close to them, his snout brushing the ground and sniffing all the smells he hasn't been exposed to living in the suburbs. Matt smiles at his dog. He's six years old. Matt got him for his tenth birthday. Old enough to listen, young enough to make this kind of journey. He couldn't have left him behind. When Silver's mother was taken, and his visits to the Melody apartment complex were limited, Einstein was there to comfort him. Silver claimed it was the dog she missed spending time with more than him. He chuckles as he walks, going through the memories, refusing to let any of the bad ones invade. Silver is his world. Always has been. And he never realized how much until Diana died. Not just because they lost a person they both cared about, but because of her visceral reaction, because of her passion, because of her thirst for justice, showcasing to Matt all the things he values in her. Their shared principles.

But he never said anything. Not about his true feelings. Not because he didn't want to, and not because he wasn't brave enough, but because they are still teenagers. Matt would spend the rest of his life with Silver. But he has a better chance of making that successful if he bides his time. Waits until they are older. Until she's gotten some experience. Had her heart broken a time or two. Then he plans to swoop in and be *that person* for her. But now...this. Part of him regrets not coming clean under the willow tree yesterday. Part of him is thankful for keeping it to himself, because if he laid all that on her, and they never saw each other again...he doesn't want her to live with that. The not knowing. And he wouldn't be able to cope with it either. So here he is, trudging through a hot and sticky forest with his family, trying to stay alive.

THE GROWL COMES out of nowhere, somewhere to Matt's right—a tremendously vicious roar that fills his blood with ice. His mom grips the machete tightly while his dad ushers Megan forward. Sofia trails behind with Einstein.

Einstein darts to Matt's side, his hackles raised, yapping up a storm. Sofia takes to the air, her wings beating furiously, keeping her ten feet above Matt's head. Smart.

The growl deepens, grows expectant. Matt tenses, his mind racing through potential escape routes. They can't outrun any four-legged creatures in these woods. The only option is to climb a tree. He calculates how long it would take to get Megan to safety. *Too long.*

Matt glances at his sister. She grips the arms of her chair so tightly her knuckles turn white. Her gaze meets his, an apology glistening in her eyes. This is not her fault. She can't think like that. He moves to shield her from whatever is coming.

Einstein backs into a bush, his warning yaps taking on an

eerie quality. Matt's eyes flick to the machete in his mom's hand. She's over ten feet away. He'll never make it. Instead, he watches her grit her teeth, plant her feet, and raise the machete high. He didn't know she had it in her.

He blinks. An enormous brown mass of fur barrels out of the undergrowth, clipping Matt's shoulder, taking his legs out from under him, spinning him in a circle. His Mom brings down the machete, but the brown creature is already streaking past them, an indescribable hulking mass of snarling jowls, sharp fangs, and murderous eyes.

Growls follow in its wake, shaking the leaves off trees and shuddering the ground. It is enormous. Whatever it is, and Matt is glad he can only see the back of it. He remains on the ground until the path ahead falls quiet.

Einstein backs into a shrub, a pitiful whine trembling past his jowls. Megan is screaming. Sofia soars higher than the canopy. His Mom grips the machete like a baseball bat, staring at the spot where the creature disappeared. His Dad is draped over Megan.

Matt pushes himself to his feet, dusts himself off, cocks his head to listen for the creature's return. But everything is silent. Well, as silent as it can be in a forest during high summer. The tension in the air is palpable, each second stretched thin with anticipation.

"What was that?" Sofia sits on a branch ten feet above his head, both arms wrapped around the trunk.

Matt checks himself for injuries, a few scratches and a throbbing shoulder, but other than that, he's in one piece. "I have no idea."

"I think it was a hellhound," Megan says.

The words drip ice down Matt's spine. They all stare at her.

"A hell *what*?" His dad keeps his eyes trained on the broken ferns the creature made during its ambush.

"A hellhound." Megan's eyes are bright with unshed tears.

Matt frowns. "I've never heard of it. No one in the resistance has mentioned it."

"I heard someone talking about it at school," Megan says. "Remember Curtis Brown?"

"That kid who's dad is part of Bear's security force?" his dad asks.

The same kid who had bullied Megan since first grade. Even more after her accident. And worse still, when he found out that her older brother was best friends with *the Silver Melody*. Daughter of the country's most treasonous criminal. Typical alt mentality.

"Yeah," Megan says. "Overheard him talking recently about these modified...dogs that the elite security forces are starting to use."

"That wasn't a dog," his mom says. "That was...that was..."

"A hellhound," Matt mutters.

"For what?" his dad asks. "What could they possible want something that vicious for?"

Megan shrugs. "Didn't hear that part."

"For tracking down the unadjusteds," Matt says. "They knew we'd run when they announced the enforced nanite program. They had to have something ready to help them enforce it."

"Enforce it or..." his mom trails off.

They all fall quiet as they contemplate the enormity of not only Megan's information, but the implications for the rest of their journey. If hellhounds are part of the security forces used to round up unadjusteds on the run...they don't stand a chance. But the hellhound ran right past them, as if it couldn't care less about them, as if it was on the scent of something in particular. *Silver*. Shit. Was the helicopter this morning responsible for dropping off hellhounds and soldiers to track down the Melodys?

"What do we do if it comes back?" Sofia asks from the tree.

"Let's not borrow from tomorrow's problems," his mom says. She and Claus are going to get along great.

"What about today's?" Megan asks.

"We've got the machete." Matt takes it from his mother. He's no more skilled than his mom, but his little sister needs her parents, and Matt feels better at the head of the group. Pushing forward. Setting a fast pace. Because...hellhounds. They need to get to safety.

Matt coaxes Einstein out of the bush and leads the small, wary group. His Dad pushes Megan's chair over weeds and roots, almost throwing her out of it a couple times. His Mom stays at the back, frequently glancing over her shoulder. It takes Sofia an hour to come out of the air and fold her wings away. Not because she's no longer scared, but because her wings are fatigued.

No one talks. They can't pretend this is a fun summer camping trip anymore. When they first entered the forest, after having escaped the mayhem of the city streets, the forest felt like a haven. But the presence of the hellhound has reminded them how much danger is still out there. That they haven't left all their problems behind with the city lights and gray concrete. That they really are on the run. For their lives.

Matt follows the crisscrossing stream, frequently refilling their water flasks, using the time spent on his knees scanning the forest as far as he can see. But they are in the thickest part, where Megan's wheels barely fit between trees, where hordes of insects feast on them, and the discordant birdsong gives him a headache.

He tenses when he hears the *whop-whop-whop* of distant helicopter blades. Are they picking up or dropping off? It's not nearby, but judging by their experience with the hellhound, the mutated creatures have a rapidity beyond any speedster. Faster than anything Matt's seen before. Maybe faster than a cheetah. He reckons they've got stamina too. Of course they do. If the scientists are going to modify a species, enhance it for a security and tracking role, of course it will have increased strength *and* speed *and* power.

Fear rolls through him, a physical wave of tension that makes his hands shake. He takes a moment, easing a deep breath into his lungs, then pushes the fear away. *Shut it down.* He has to stop thinking, keep moving, push it all away. That's the only way he's going to get through.

The descending darkness a couple of hours later hits Matt by surprise. According to his compass and his own mental map, they are ahead of schedule. Maybe it was the hellhound that gave them all a burst of increased energy. He glances at the trees, wondering if they could spend the night in the thick branches. With the birds and the chipmunks. But he doesn't have enough rope to secure them all safety. They will have to risk the ground, build a better shelter, and be vigilant about keeping watch.

Sofia volunteers to go first. She does it from a branch twenty feet above their heads with just the flashlight for company. Matt keeps his hand on the machete while he sleeps. When his dad wakes him for his turn at watch just before dawn, he's surprised he's slept. With the machete strapped to his belt, he fills all the water flasks and packs as much as he can while he waits for his family to rouse.

The following day and night are a repeat of the same. Tension never leaves Matt's body. Words are sparse between them. Sofia keeps to the air as much as she can. It isn't until their fourth day on the run that the landscape shifts a little. Wooden structures come into view late afternoon. A smattering of dilapidated houses, most of their roofs caved in, stone chimneys crumbling, a disused well in the center of it all. They won't stop here for the night. Many forest paths lead to and from this location. It was one they used for a camping spot several years ago. The army could be using it as a base. They and their hellhound hunt dogs.

Matt shudders as they walk by, but catches a burst of movement. He stills, raises a hand to the rest of his family to be quiet. There it is again. A flash of dark green against a dark green background. Something moving past one of the missing planks inside one of the houses.

"Everyone, get back," he hisses.

Sofia flies into a tree. His Mom wheels Megan into a bush. Einstein follows.

His dad stands by his side, whispers in his ear. "I got your back."

Matt nods, tightens his grip on the machete, attempts to ignore the uneven gallop of his heart. Dark green. Could be army. Could be someone in camouflage. Could be a whole world of things. He doesn't hear any growls. But that doesn't mean hellhounds aren't nearby. They could be leashed and muzzled. Although how the hell someone can leash a creature with that kind of strength...

"Matt..." his dad warms as the movement becomes more solid. Matt tracks the dark green thing through the ruined planks, watching it advance to the open front door area. Any minute now, they'll see who, or what, it is.

CHAPTER 7

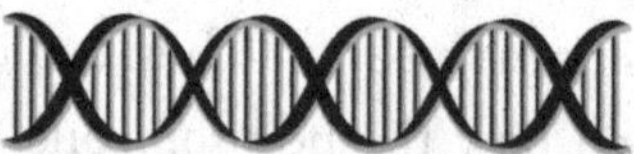

THE POSSIBILITIES BARREL through Matt's head as the figure emerges from the ruined structure. Are they caught? Is it all over? Will they be stuck in a compound? Will they find Lyla?

The figure smiles at him and Matt's shoulders drop in relief.

"Isn't that your Social Studies teacher?" his dad asks.

Mrs. Montoya. Francesca.

"Yep." Matt smiles as Francesa lowers her raised hands and smiles right back at him. "She's one of the leaders of the resistance."

His dad lets out a low whistle. Matt gestures for his family to come out of hiding. Einstein is the first to emerge and he closes the gap between Matt and Francesca, gives her a good sniffing, then lets out a single bark of approval.

They meet by the well, Matt and Francesca looking each other up and down. She wears green hiking trousers and a green T-shirt, blending in well with the forest. He's never seen her in anything but a skirt before. Matt smiles at the leaves and pine needles in her thick, dark hair, the grime encrusted under her chipped fingernails.

"Everything okay?" he asks, as his family crowds around them.

Francesca releases a frustrated sigh. "Claus took a bullet on the way here—"

"He's okay, right?" Matt's pulse increases. Claus. One of their leaders. With a vast amount of military and combat experience...they need him. Silver needs him.

"He's okay," Francesa says. "It didn't hit anything important. Straight in and out. I did my best to stich him up, but progress is slow."

Matt looks past her at the derelict house Claus must be resting inside of. Maybe he and Megan can both ride in the wheelchair? But they'd be too heavy to push.

"We can take a break inside," Matt says to his family. "Grab a quick nap. But we can't spend the night here."

"But it has walls," Sofia says.

Barely.

"We used to come here all the time." Megan's gaze skims the circle of old homes, her features softening. "I remember that one has a beautiful brick hearth with a wide seat in front for warming your hands...or making s'mores."

"That's right," Matt says, allowing his mind to relax into the memories.

The group makes their way into the wooden house. Claus is laid out on a roll mat, his weight propped up by one elbow.

"Matt," Claus says, then raises a brow when the rest of the group enters. "And the Lawson family...and..." he smiles at Sofia, her pinks wings are a startling contrast to the greens and browns of the forest.

"Sofia," she says quietly.

"It's nice to meet you, Sofia," Claus says in his welcoming yet authoritative way that puts everyone at ease.

His Mom wheels Megan over the broken floorboards to the side of a burned hearth, while his dad coaxes Sofia further into the house. Einstein gives Claus a once over, wagging his tail as if he's found a prize.

Matt and Francesca kneel on the floor by Claus.

"How bad is it?" Matt asks.

Claus' face remains neutral. "Not so bad, but I can't walk on it much. Not yet."

"We can't stay here," Matt says.

"Francesca was about to go and find a branch for a crutch," Claus says.

"People are going to be waiting for us at the cave," Matt says. "People who have no idea what to do next."

"You go on ahead," Francesca says. "You can welcome them."

Matt shakes his head. "We're just as slow as you. And besides, I'm not leaving you two. We're safer in a group."

Claus offers his hand for Matt to shake. "You are a fine young man, Mr. Lawson."

Matt blushes, but takes the offered hand. "That's quite a compliment coming from you." He turns to Francesca. "Is there anyone on your tail?"

She shakes her head. "It was a guard who got us as we ran

for my car. I got him back." She lifts the hem of her T-shirt to reveal a handgun nestled into the waistband of her trousers. Matt's eyes widen. Guns are another thing he has a problem with, but if they're about to fight a war, they're going to need firepower. And lots of it.

"I'm glad you're both okay," he says, looking between their stern faces. "I can't do this without you."

Francesca claps his back. "You're capable of more than you realize."

"I'm sixteen."

"Age is just a number," Claus says. "You have an old soul inside you." He touches Matt's chest. The gesture feels both oddly intimate and reassuring. Claus moves his hand to Matt's head. "And an excellent brain resting in there too."

If Lyla was here, she'd warn Claus that Matt's ego was in danger of over inflating. Her absence brings a sudden tightening to his chest.

"Have you heard anything about compounds?" Matt asks.

"Unadjusteds are being rounded up," Francesca says. "Bear suspected the behavior of the altereds would turn... difficult, without the presence of the unadjusteds. So he planned to round up unadjusteds at the same time as rolling out the enforced nanite program."

"You knew about the God Factor? You knew about the compounds?" Matt asked.

Francesca shook her head. "Not until a few days ago. A friend of mine from the campaign trail got word to me. But it didn't give us time to prepare."

"Bear is going to round all the unadjusteds up, keep them in compounds across the country to even out the murderous impulses of the altereds who have ingested multiple nanites," Claus says.

"Including himself," Matt adds.

"Including himself," Francesca echoes.

"How can he roll out an enforced nanite program if unadjusteds are needed to keep them all sane?" Megan asks from a few feet away.

Matt didn't realize she was listening. He turns to face her. "Because you can still take one or two nanites without gaining those murderous impulses. And if you keep to nanites that aren't harnessed from animals or don't change your physical appearance, there's no risk. At least, that's how Rufus explained it."

"I told you it was more powerful being an unadjusted," Megan says, and the whole room turns to look at her. His little sister, who may have an older soul than him, and probably a bigger brain too.

"Power is in the mind," Claus says, tapping his temple. "Not out here." He gestures to his body. "You are quite right, young lady, and I am proud to be making the rest of the journey with you."

Megan beams, then gives Matt a knowing look. His little sister, ladies and gentlemen.

While the others eat packaged food, Matt pushes himself off the floor and heads outside with Einstein and the machete. They have a couple hours of daylight left, enough time to get away from the village and find a safer shelter for the night. But first Matt spends ten minutes selecting a couple of sturdy branches, Einstein sniffing his approval of each one, and then carves them into crutches. One end blunt

Claus can put under his arm, the other whittled into a fine point that can be used as a weapon. Claus may not have the use of one leg, but Matt has seen what he can do with just his hands. The crutches will be more than enough weapon for him, if needed.

Matt returns inside and helps Claus to his feet, gives him one crutch and the other to his mother to use as a spear. His father will push the wheelchair. Francesca will take up the rear with her handgun, Matt will lead the group with the machete. Sofia hovers in the middle somewhere, usually close to Megan.

Claus and his mother walk together. He hears them talking, getting to know each other, exchanging information about what they know. Even though Claus is injured, Matt feels a hell of a lot safer with him in the group. He is not a black-belt-master-dan-level-whatever for no reason. And the reassurance of the presence of Francesca's gun can't be denied, no matter how much he hates them.

They walk for close to two hours before darkness impedes their progress. After they set up camp for the night and divide food, Matt and Francesa venture toward the stream to freshen up.

"Have you been hearing helicopters?" Matt asks.

Francesa nods. "Means there are more unadjusteds on the run than they anticipated." She scans his face, then adds. "That's a *good* thing, Matt."

"Not if they all get caught. Not if they get killed by hell-hounds. Not if Silver and Rufus are out there." He finally gives voice to his worries and can't help them tumbling out of him. Around his family, he's kept them buttoned down. But this is Francesca. A co-leader of the resistance. Over the last few months, they've spoken many times about the potential risks and outcomes. Francesca has always been reassuring. But then, she has no family to worry about.

Matt splashes water over his face and combs it through his tangled hair. Repeats the process a couple times as if the water can wash the fear away. It sits there, hovering below the surface, always threatening to rear its ugly head and immobilize him.

Francesca puts a hand on his shoulder. "Silver is going to be okay."

"You don't know that."

"No, I don't. But I feel it. She's resourceful."

A beat of silence passes between them as cicadas chirp from the undergrowth and ants wriggle past his boots.

"And if she doesn't make it to the cave, then she doesn't make it to the cave."

Matt's head snaps in her direction. He glares at her in the filtered moonlight. "How can you say that?"

Francesca's features soften. "You can't control her future. Nor yours, or mine, or anyone's heading to the cave. What will be will be. We're damn well going to fight for it...but we can't get twisted up in the things we can't control."

Her words make sense, but he hates every single one of them. "I can't...I can't do this without her."

The hand on his shoulder squeezes. "You will if you have to."

"But we need Rufus."

"We do. But if we don't get him, then we find another way."

Matt feels like he's been punched by a bulk. "I don't think you understand. Silver...she's always been there for me...when Diana died..." he can't put it into words. The emotion is too much. There aren't the words to express everything he feels.

"I have people in my life like that too," she says softly.

"You do? Are they coming to the cave?"

"That remains to be seen."

They finish filling the flasks in silence, but the weight on Matt's chest is now tighter and heavier. Breathing is hard. Harder than hard. It's so freaking humid in the forest and he's always sweating and now tears are mingling with the water running down his face. He dragged his family out here, into the wild, to find a sanctuary that may or may not keep them safe. They put their trust in him. *Shit.*

Francesca doesn't comment, but sits next to him as he pulls himself together. He's the leader of a resistance and here he is sitting by a stream in the forest at midnight crying. He tells himself it's because he cares so much. And he does. Of course he does. Of course he wants things to be fair for the unadjusteds. But he's also got to keep his family safe. And Silver. He promised her a way out.

Shut it down.

A bark from Einstein alerts Matt that something isn't right. Matt leaps to his feet, listening to Einstein's low growls. Growls of warning. Then comes a scream. Sofia.

Abandoning the water flasks, Matt runs back to the campsite only a five-minute walk away. Now it feels like miles. Francesca is close on his heels, her gun in her hand, safety off. The screaming doesn't stop. And now other shouts reverberate through the forest. And barking.

Matt jumps over ferns, ducks under low-hanging branches, and peels around the corner of a towering oak tree. As the campsite comes into view, ice coats Matt's skin, clamps his neck in a frigid grip. He skids over soil and pinecones, putting the brakes on so he doesn't slide into the jaws of a terrifying creature. A wolf. Its back as high as Matt's shoulders, its jaws clamped around Sofia's wing.

Einstein growls at the wolf, receiving only a menacing snarl from the animal as it refuses to release Sofia's wing. Megan huddles in a corner with his mom. His dad holds the machete, but by the look on his face, has no idea what to do with it. Claus raises his crutch, the pointy end aimed at the wolf's eyes. But it is so big. So powerful. Genetically enhanced in all the worst possible ways. And probably human.

Matt doesn't stop running, but barrels into the animal's flank, his momentum forcing the wolf to let go of Sofia. It isn't a clean wound. Teeth tear through the pink, chitinous material, shredding the delicate fibers, and the wolf is knocked into the back of the shelter. Cornered.

They both come to a stop. Matt is on the ground, on his side. The wolf is on all fours, saliva from its vicious mouth dripping all over him, luminous eyes pinning him to the earth.

Matt swallows. The wolf growls. Gunshots sound. Three in quick succession. He feels the heat of one whizz by his ear.

The wolf stares at him a moment longer. Then, without

warning, with its eyes still wide and murderous, drops over on its side. Dead.

Matt doesn't release his breath. The monster always comes back. But that doesn't happen this time. This time, the body of the wolf morphs into something else. As they all stare, what remains is the muscly body of a human male in his mid-twenties, three bullet holes piercing his chest.

CHAPTER 8

SOFIA IS UNCONSCIOUS.

As his dad drags the body of the wolf/man out of the shelter and behind a nearby tree, Matt and his mom crouch by Sofia's side. He digs out a first aid kit and rummages through it, but there is nothing inside that can help a shredded wing.

His mom takes a strip of bandage out of his hands. "Her shoulder is dislocated. I'm going to need this to make a sling once I get it back in place."

Matt raises an eyebrow. "You know how to do that?"

His mom grits her teeth. "On an animal." His mom is a receptionist at a veterinary clinic. Was. She picked up a few things along the way. For animals.

"You can do it, Mom," Megan says.

"I'd help," Claus says. "But I won't be able to get the purchase with my bad leg."

"It's okay." Mom flashes him a tight smile. "I can do this."

"Best to do it now, while she's still unconscious," Claus says, a hand running through his thickening mustache.

His Mom nods, glances at Matt. He gives her his best reassuring face.

"Hold her here," his mom says. "And here."

Matt obliges, averting his gaze from the teeth marks and trickles of blood running down her arm. Her shredded wing. There's barely anything left of it, just scraps of bright pink curled into ribbons of nothingness.

His Mom moves quick, with a rapid snap of her hands, shoving the shoulder back into its socket. Sofia's eyes fly open. She lets out a piercing scream. One that Matt is sure will attract every animal in a nearby radius. And there are things in the forest far worse than modified wolves. Hellhounds, for one.

His Mom folds Sofia into her arms, rocks her like a baby. Matt can only sit on his knees and watch. Megan shifts through the first aid kit, starts swabbing Sofia's arm with an antibacterial cleaner as her screams dissipate and become whimpers.

Using his crutch, Claus pushes himself to his feet, glances at the clouded sky through the dark canopy.

His dad drops the machete at Matt's side. "It's all yours, son. I don't think I can..."

Matt gets to his feet. "It's okay dad."

"We don't have the means to bury the man," Claus says. They glance at the corpse where his feet stick out from under a bush. "Nor should we spend the energy on it. And it's going to attract every predator and scavenger for miles around. We can't stay here tonight."

"Agreed," his dad says and starts rolling sleeping bags and shoving them into packs.

"It's pitch black," Matt says to Claus. "Can't see a damn thing."

"So we use a flashlight," Claus says. "It's better than sticking around here."

"I'll take the flashlight," Francesca says. "So I can use it with my gun. It'll keep us safe."

Matt doesn't mention an attack could come from any direction, not just the one Francesca happens to be looking in. But they don't have a choice.

Once Sofia has quietened and been fed a handful of painkillers, they all get to their feet and hoist packs onto shoulders.

After Matt retrieves the flasks from the stream, Francesca leads the way with the flashlight and gun. His dad pushes Megan behind her. Sofia leans on his mom as they trip through the undergrowth. And Matt, with the machete, walks at the back of the group with Claus and Einstein. At least the dog will give them a heads up if anything is coming.

Matt's heart thrums uncomfortably in his chest as they shuffle through the undergrowth. He swishes at the bushes with the machete, hacking the heads off ferns and shrubs, wishing he could defeat the altereds as easily.

But it's not really the bushes he's attacking. Or the altereds. It's his control. Or lack of it. For all the plans he made, getting supplies to the caves, getting through the forest, ensuing Silver and her dad came when they could...he never pictured doing any of it without his best friend. Not that they could journey together, but being in the forest, coming face to face with hellhounds and modified wolves and the sounds of aggressive helicopters...fear catches up to him. There is no guarantee that everything will go his way. Life isn't always fair. He learned that early on when he had to be saved at birth from a brain defect. Again, when Silver's mom was taken. Again, when Megan was in the car wreck. And now again with the enforced nanite program. And all the small stuff in between. He's never been hung up on it before. There is nothing he can do to change the past or alter what's coming. He can only prepare. But dammit, he didn't count on the fear being this physical, living and breathing monster that blows down his neck with every step he takes. Because every step he takes toward the cave, feels like a step further away from Silver.

He's seen Silver have an anxiety attack. He knows how bad they are for her. Wishes he could do something to take them away. She won't make it through the woods without having one or two. But she'll still come. She'll still fight. Even against herself. Until they are together again. And that is one of the reasons he loves her. Because she fights, even when she doesn't think she can. Even if she goes a little violent. They're going to need that.

Einstein presses against his leg, looks up at Matt with his soulful brown eyes. Matt switches the machete to the other hand and gives the dog a rough scrunch behind the ears, eliciting a groan that makes him smile.

Matt hears the flapping of wings. Large wings. There aren't birds big enough in the forest to cause that kind of noise, or to cause that kind of gust against his face. He raises the machete as Claus balances on one leg and raises the crutch. They both look up.

In the darkness, it's hard to make out the large object tunneling toward them from under the canopy. Until Francesca catches it in the cone of the flashlight and follows it as it...falls.

Wings and arms and legs in a wild windmill of chaos arrow toward the ground. Matt and Claus step out of the way, weapons raised. Nothing with wings is ever good. Unless it's Sofia. Matt admonishes himself for the unkind thoughts about altereds with wings. Think of Diana. It's not what they've taken, but how they came by their change, and how they feel about it now. Diana taught him to never judge a person or alt by their appearance. Being an altered is a mentality. Even the purest of unadjusteds, who have never taken a nanite, can be the worst kind of alts.

A scream comes from the bundle of wings and limbs. Francesca keeps the light trained on the descent, as well as the gun.

"Oof."

The figure smacks into a thick branch, performs a haphazard circle around its girth, and falls out the other way, slower this time.

"Oof." The figure hits the ground.

After a few seconds of stillness, Matt and Claus dare to approach. Claus pokes an array of bright green feathers with his stick. The figure moves, heaving in a rasping breath. Then a face peers from beneath a wing. "Don't shoot."

The eyes are as green as the wings. Brighter. Glowing in

the darkness. Long, tangled hair cascades past her waist. She raises her hands. "Don't shoot."

Francesca edges closer, both her gun and light in the girl's face, making her slit her eyes. "Who are you?"

The girl shakes her shoulders and an assortment of leaves and twigs and pine needles fall out of her wings. "I'm Paige."

"What are you doing here, Paige?" Claus asks.

Paige looks back up at the tree she fell out of. "Was trying to sleep. Something bit me. And I am not a fan of bugs, or rodents or whatever else might be in that tree. Or those horrible dogs and wolves running around the ground—"

"Hellhounds?" Megan leans forward in her chair.

"Is that what they are?" Paige shudders. "Well, I was in the middle of a dream, about fishing on the river way back home, and fell right out of that tree."

Matt can't hide his smile. "You didn't think to use your wings?"

Paige lowers her hands. "I have a twelve-foot wingspan. No way I could extend them up there. In here."

"Fair point," Matt responds.

"Where are you going?" Francesca asks.

"I wasn't going anywhere. I was sleeping."

Francesa edges closer. "Are you saying you live in the forest?"

Matt gives her a once over. Despite the leaves and twigs adhered to her hair and wings, she doesn't look like she's been living rough.

"It's a free country," Paige retorts.

Matt scoffs. "Is it?"

"Maybe not anymore." Paige gets to her feet, narrows her bright green eyes. "I don't have to tell you anything."

"I'm the one with the gun." Francesa waves it in her face.

Matt edges around his ex-teacher. Passion runs strong in her blood, and while he admires her tenacity and determination, now is the time for prudence.

He plasters what he hopes is a reassuring smile on his face. All the time he is aware of the darkness at their backs, the sounds their voices make in the otherwise silent night.

"It's hard to trust anyone," Matt says, gesturing to where his mom stands with her arm around Sofia. He points to Sofia's undamaged wing. "We all feel a little like that."

"Wait, I thought you were all unadjusteds?" Paige says, scanning our small group.

"Most of us are," Claus says. "But that doesn't mean we're defenseless."

"No, of course not," Paige says, appraising the stern expression on his face. "Where are you all going?"

Now that Francesca has moved the spotlight away from Paige's face, he can take in her appearance. There's the long dark hair and emerald eyes, the green wings. She looks to be a year or two older than himself. A sense of kindness rolls off her. Matt's always prided himself on being a good judge of character, but his emotions are all over the place right now. And maybe his judgement too. She appears to be on her own. Unless this is a trap.

"You first," Matt says.

Paige chews on her lip, plucks a few leaves out of her wings. "Okay. I'm trusting you..."

"And we you." Francesca gestures with the gun.

Paige zeroes in on it, her teeth digging deeper into her lip.

Matt puts his hand on the barrel of the gun and urges Francesca to lower it. "She's unarmed."

"How can you tell? She could have any number of weapons hidden within those wings." Francesca doesn't put the gun away, but she flicks the safety on.

Paige raises her hands once more, shakes her wings, extends them as far as she can while Francesca combs the flashlight over them. It's five minutes until she is satisfied.

"A friend of mine told me about a safe place to go," Paige says. "Where unadjusteds are gathering—"

"You're not an unadjusted," Francesca says.

"No," Paige admits. "But I wish I was. The wings..." she gives them a cursory glance. "Let's just say I went about it all wrong...I have regrets...and I don't think anyone should be forced into taking a nanite...my parents..." Her voice cracks. She dips her chin. "Sorry, that's another story for another time. I have a habit of talking when I'm nervous. My friend told me about a cave where people are gathering. A resistance. A place where we can learn to fight back."

Matt smiles. "That's where we're going too." He steps forward and offers his hand. Introduces himself and the rest of the group.

"Would you like to join us, or would you feel safer on your own?" his mother asks.

"We could use someone to scout ahead from the air," Claus says.

"I'd very much like to join you if you'll have me," Paige says, folding her wings away.

"Are you on your own?" Megan asks.

Paige nods, her eyes glistening once more. "My parents... let's just say we see things differently."

"I'm sorry," Matt says, for the first time realizing how many families will split over this divide. How many irreparable bridges will be burned.

"Did you guys hear about the compounds? And the price on the Melody's heads?" Paige asks as they adjust to each other's company.

Matt's lungs seize and he is in danger of face-planting the hard-baked ground. "Price? There's a price on their heads?"

Paige nods. "A million each. Alive."

CHAPTER 9

HE COULD GO BACK. Hike through the forest, run through the city, all the way to Silver's apartment. But if she's done what she promised, she won't be there. Her father and her will be on the run. In the same forest Matt now stands, holding his breath, not daring to move. Moving means action. Action means he will have made a decision. And he can't turn his back on Silver. But he has no idea where she is.

A million dollars. Each. *Alive.*

Thank God for small miracles. They want them alive. But what if they capture Rufus? Will Silver become collateral damage? After all, she is unadjusted, merely the daughter of two great scientists, one of them a traitor.

"Silver." Matt breathes her name on an exhale, and it hurts, like his lungs and throat are filled with razor blades. Paige is staring at him. Her mouth opening and closing, but he can' t hear her, can only hear the booming of his own rushing pulse.

"Matt?" His Mom's hand is on his shoulder. He turns his head to look at her. "Matt? Are you okay?"

"Silver," he whispers again, the second time equally as painful.

"She's a red belt in karate," Megan reminds him.

And she's violent. But is a red belt and violence enough against a bulk or a hellhound?

"You know the Melodys?" Paige asks, her mouth gaping open.

Matt doesn't answer, doesn't confirm or deny. Is a million dollars enough to turn Paige against them?

"She's in a safe place," Claus tells Paige. "Out of the city, far away from here." Looks Like Claus is having trust issues too.

"That's good," Paige says. Fiddling with a feather that fell out of her wing. "I hope they stay safe. Together. I wish my parents had...never mind."

"She's my best friend," Matt says. He keeps his other feelings to himself. They are his and his alone.

"A million dollars is a lot of money," Francesa says, placing the gun back in the waistband of her trousers.

Thanks for the reminder.

"Rufus is pretty smart too, you know," his dad says. "He told me about his temporary nanites. Stuff that cloaks your scent, blends you in with your background for short periods of time—"

"Wait, they're going to take nanites to escape nanites?" Megan asks.

The irony isn't lost on any of them. And not if Silver has a say in it. She won't. Matt remembers the time she was tempted. But that was before Diana. Now, Silver is one of the most ani-alt people he knows. Rufus is going to have a hell of a time getting her to take a nanite, even if it is temporary. It goes against everything that's important to her, everything she stands for, everything her mom got thrown in prison for. But she may have no choice. And that's where things get gray.

It's the mentality, Matt reminds himself. It doesn't matter if Silver takes a couple of temporary nanites to save her own life. It's the mentality that counts. She will never be an alt.

If anyone is an alt in their relationship, it's him. He's the one that had extra intelligence during the surgery while he was still cooking inside his mom. Although there was no nanite involved, and Rufus manipulated his DNA in vitro... it's still *altered*. Maybe that's why he is so careful to give the altereds a chance to join the resistance. So many of them are unhappy with their nanites, with their abilities, with how they are...treated. *Try being an unadjusted.*

He remembers the pro football player who recently got dropped. A bulk. One of the highest tiered nanites and most expensive. His story spread across the country. Only a couple years older than Matt, saved up all his money to buy the nanite, got his knee wrecked during his first season and his insurance didn't cover the regeneration nanite. No more football. Last he heard; the player was on his way to Central City to plead his case. He's been pretty outspoken about the whole thing. Some of the more pro alt networks refused to show his interviews. Who knows what's happened to him now. And that's just one example.

"You have to do what you have to do," Paige says to Megan. "Some people think the world is black and white.

Others that it's a range of gray. Really, it's a rainbow, and viewpoints shift all the time. If your friend needs to take a few temporary nanites to survive...then that's what she has to do. Especially during times of..."

"War," Matt finishes for her. It's a tough word to speak aloud. Looking at how humanity has overcome a myriad of obstacles in its history, to be faced with a civil war over super-powers...he shakes his head. Sometimes he feels like he's living in a sci-fi novel.

"War," Paige repeats. The trembling in her wings doesn't escape Matt's notice.

Even though they've been walking most of the night, they carry on when the sun rises. They can't afford to be caught by a roaming troop of bulk soldiers or a hellhound with a scent up its nose. If they truly are hunting Silver and Rufus, it's not a leap to think that Matt and his family will also be people of interest. Their relationship with the Melody family is well documented. The Lawson family home has welcomed bulk security guards into their residence on more than one occasion, mainly to be informed of what the rules are surrounding the Melodys.

As Matt walks, hacking at the ferns with the machete, all he can see in his mind are dollar signs. Right next to Silver's beautiful face. But, he tells himself, the money doesn't change anything. They were being hunted before, and they are being hunted now. Most civilians won't have a clue how to find them or where the cave is. And Matt would bet a lot of money on the fact that no one in the resistance would turn her in. They all want the same goal. Change. A ban on nanites. Respect for unadjusted life.

But would he turn down one million dollars for it? His throat thickens and he coughs around the roughness. Then pushes the thoughts away, concentrates on planting foot after foot, hacking the path clear for Megan, even though they're leaving an obvious trail, but they don't have a choice. And if he focuses on the sweat ribboning down his spine, on avoiding the roots threatening to trip him up, even picturing the coolness of the lake in the cave, then maybe he'll stop worrying for more than two seconds. No guarantees, though. Maybe it's a side effect of the increased intelligence. A heightened ability to picture all the outcomes, good and bad, and the subsequent energy spent on making plans to avoid each negative outcome. It's exhausting. But it is one of the reasons he was chosen to help lead the resistance.

For their last night in the woods, after Paige helps move Megan and Claus into the branches of a tall tree, they lash them to the trunk so neither will fall out. The rest of them who are more mobile roll out the sleeping bags on the ground. Paige wedges herself into a gap between two branches near his sister, promises to keep an eye on her. Wearily, Matt nods at her as she settles in and whispers to Megan. He is glad they ran into her. Whenever they heard helicopters during the day, Paige scaled the trees and flew above the canopy to check out the situation. Each time she came back with a report, informing them the helicopters were far away, easing their tension. She's made the remainder of the journey far less stressful.

Afraid to lie on the ground, Sofia sleeps curled in Megan's wheelchair, protecting her bandaged arm. Matt lies on the end of the row of sleeping bags, the machete in his hand, Einstein nestled into his side. Then it's his dad, his mom, Paige and Francesca. She sleeps with the gun under her head. Matt can't make up his mind if that's a good thing or a bad thing. But he's too tired to worry about it.

His dad nudges him awake when the sun is already high in the sky. Matt blinks against the intrusive brightness. "You should have woken me."

"You needed the sleep," his dad says.

Matt gets to his feet to find the rest of the camp packed. Paige hands him the machete. Einstein licks his hand. Before they set off, Matt splashes water on his face and takes a long sip. His stomach gurgles for something more substantial than trail mix and package food, but it's going to be a long time until he sits down to a three-course meal.

Despite the niggly aches and pains, scratches and bruises Matt's accrued during the hike, undercurrents of excitement flash through him occasionally. According to his mental map and the compass, they will reach the cave by midafternoon. He sees the recognition on Francesca's and Claus' faces too. A brightening of their eyes, a release of the tension bracketing their mouths, a softening of features.

"Can we stop for water?" his mom asks an hour later. Matt chucks her his water bottle.

An hour after that, they come across a small cluster of people searching through an area of dense foliage.

Francesca removes her gun, Matt clenches the machete. But Paige's face lights up with a smile. She puts a hand on Matt's arm. "I know them. They're the ones who told me about the cave."

"They're looking in the wrong place," Matt says.

They meet up with the group, and after exchanging pleasantries and determining they are who they say they are, they join together and hike the rest of the way to the cave. Through a clearing awash with wildflowers of every color, then onto a ridge overlooking a wide valley. They stand on the ridge, peering into the valley below, at the small copse of trees which hide the entrance to the cave. The path is wide open to the sky. If a helicopter flies by...but they have no choice.

One by one, they step over the ridgeline and into the valley, some running, some walking, his dad pushing Megan's chair. Claus performs a fast limp, with his mom guiding him down the shallowest gradient.

Twenty minutes later, they arrive at the small thicket of trees and shrubs. Matt's chest lifts. Two years of planning culminates in this moment.

There is a hushed expectancy from the people at his back. Francesca nudges his arm. "Go on."

Matt pulls away branches from a concealed door half sunk in the ground. You wouldn't know it is there unless you are looking for it. Then he yanks the door open to see a mouth of darkness.

Paige peers inside, gives him a doubtful look.

"It stinks," Megan says.

"You'll get used to it," Matt tells her. But it doesn't stink. It's the damp clay and limestone, the scent of ancient and old things, a thread of fresh water. But the strongest scent is freedom.

CHAPTER 10

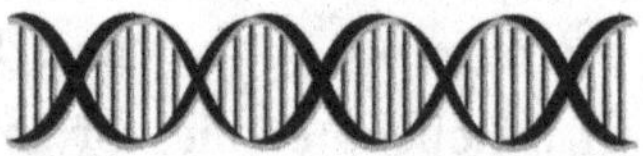

MATT STRETCHES his arm inside the dark entrance and turns on an LED lantern. The cave lights up, revealing twenty yards of a gradual descent. The planks he previously laid down for Megan's wheelchair should make things easier for her. She'll be able to push herself around.

When he looks over his shoulder to gesture everyone to follow him inside, he notes there are now over fifty people clumped at his back. He recognizes many faces, several of those he had meetings with during the forming of the resistance. A couple push four-wheeled carts with off-road wheels carrying supplies. He spots a box of ammo, and the gleam of matte black weapons.

"This way." He leads everyone inside, flicking the lanterns on as he moves. They've been set every twenty feet along the path, several more around the main chamber. They emerge into it a few minutes later, able to straighten up, the sense of space making it easier to breathe, despite the dampness. It's as big as a football pitch. Once Matt and Francesca turn on the rest of the lanterns, he sighs with relief when he spots the boxes of food in the area they designated the kitchen. A couple of naturally occurring chimneys will allow them to smoke meat and boil water. They have enough for now. For a week or two. But the population will grow and supply runs will be needed.

Everyone dumps their stuff in the main chamber. Einstein takes a good look around, sniffing a path into all the corners, barking at things they can't see, disappearing down narrow passageways. Matt leads them on a tour through the cave. Shows them the two passages that have several niches carved into them he thought could serve as bedrooms. He's already loaded a few items into a niche for himself. As he walks by, he catches sight of the framed photo of Silver and his throat flexes with a hard swallow. *Shut it down.*

A third passageway leads to a series of large chambers that Francesa designated as offices and a lab for Rufus. If he arrives. There are boxes here too. Francesca opens one, pulls out a pad of paper and a pen, and begins taking a list of names of everyone in the cave. Ages. Abilities. Where they've come from. What strengths they may possess. She is already preparing for war.

The fourth and final passageway leads to the underground lake. Matt is tempted to fall into it, cool off, wash the dirt and grime and fear off his skin. There is a current flowing through it, an underground river that allows them to corner off a section for drinking supplies, and a different one for washing and bathing. The resistance team decided water was the most crucial element of whatever shelter they set up in, and this location couldn't provide them better. Of course, none of the proposed hideouts were perfect. They all brought their own challenges, but deep within the cool walls of the cavern, Matt feels safe. His family is safe. The first task on his list of duties is complete.

Francesca is quick to assign tasks to the gathered people. After everyone has claimed a private niche, she appoints a handful of people to go through the food boxes and prepare an evening meal. Others are allocated washing up duties. That night, they sit on old rugs with a few lanterns between them, telling their stories. Most of them are unadjusted, but there are a few in the gathering who are alts. Some have wings. A couple have increased speed. Most people are injured. Some of their companions didn't make it.

A woman in her twenties cradles a guitar, her fingers strumming tunelessly over the strings, her eyes glistening in the low light of the lanterns.

Matt offers her a handful of crackers.

She shakes her head. "I don't think I can eat right now."

"You play?" He nods at the guitar.

The woman shakes her head again and a tear drips down her cheek. "Belongs to a friend. A friend who didn't make it. I don't know what to do with it. I supposed it would make useful firewood, but I'd rather hear someone play it. Someone who knows how."

A sudden sense of rightness fills Matt's chest. "I know someone. She's on her way here. If you don't mind?"

The woman offers him a mournful smile and presses the guitar into his hands. "I'm glad to hear it. I look forward to hearing her play."

During the rest of dinner, Matt introduces himself to

everyone. No one mentions the reward money for the Melodys. He dares to hope the people here either don't care, or they were already on the run when the news broke. It eases the tension he carries at the back of his neck a little.

That night, after he and Claus and Francesca catalog every box and person—and animal, including Einstein—he makes his way to his private room. His parents and Megan found a slightly larger area for all three of them further down the passageway. They have already rolled out his sleeping bag, filled his flask with fresh water, and hung an old sheet across his archway to offer a semblance of privacy. The fairy lights he brought on a previous trip have been turned on. The gentle glow allows the cave to feel...not exactly like a home away from home, but a promise that things will be okay.

Matt puts the guitar in the corner, stares at it for a few minutes. He wants to take it as a sign that Silver will make it here, but he can't give in to sentimental or superstitious thinking. He plucks a string, the vibration moving along his finger, and wishes he knew how to play.

Barely able to keep his eyes open, he flops onto his sleeping bag, not bothering to take off his shoes, and stares at the picture of Silver. It was taken during one of his birthday parties, when she was still allowed out. They went bowling. He stuck bunny ears behind her head. It's her smile he loves the most. Full and wide, with a hint of violence. He smiles at her now. And then he falls asleep.

Day one inside the cave is spent roping people into more jobs. Kyle arrives, and he and Paige agree to scope out the immediate area to see where they can gather supplies from. Steal. Raid. Whatever.

On day two, Matt heads outside with Einstein and works on burying his bombs around the perimeter of the entrance to the cave. The sensors are voice activated or can be detonated by pressing a button on his remote control.

On day three, his parents leave the cave with Megan under his care. They plan to hunt for Lyla.

On day four, he panics. He wakes to the picture of Silver falling on his chest, scraping across his chin, and tries not to take it as a sign. If she left when he did, she should be here by now. Maybe she got delayed a day or two, but she should still be here by now, dammit.

Shut it down.

There are now four hundred people in the cave. Paige and Sawyer have been on three supply runs. They've roped in a female with butterfly wings which change color according to her emotions. And a bulk. Matt didn't expect to see a bulk join the resistance. But Hal's unadjusted wife and son were ripped away from him during the chaos. He won't talk about it, but Matt suspects their fate was worse than being thrown into a compound. There's the seven-foot-tall unadjusted female with flame-red hair who excels at throwing stars. But where the hell is Silver?

Matt ventures outside to bury more of his bombs, Einstein keeping a close eye on him, grumbling a low warning if a dragonfly gets too close. Claus is in the meadow over the ridge, setting up his training arena. It was always part of the plan. It's one thing for unadjusteds to flee the city and get to safety, but they can't live in hiding forever. At some point they will have to fight back. And they'll have to learn how to do that. That is Claus' area. Matt sticks to the bombs. And convincing people they are stronger than they think. If they thought getting to the cave was the hard part...

Einstein woofs gently beside Matt, and when he looks at the golden ball of fluff, he wags his tail. Can't be too serious. A flash of movement directs his attention to the ridge.

Shielding his eyes from the midday sun, he crouches behind a bush and scans the line of trees and shrubs. There. People. Two. Barely concealed behind a large trunk. They too are inspecting their surroundings, but their focus is on the valley floor. They must be new arrivals.

As the two figures emerge from the trees, Matt's heart beats a throb of hope. Einstein chuffs at him, telling him what he can hardly believe.

Silver. It's *Silver*, running down the slope. With a...bulk.

Matt swallows. Rufus is nowhere to be seen.

Silver and the bulk approach the copse of trees where Matt stands. He is desperate to wrap his arms around her. To pull her into his arms. To feel her body tight against his chest. But there is the...bulk.

They peer into the bushes, move a few branches out of the way. Matt decides to put them out of their misery.

"Hello, stranger."

Silver startles. The bulk raises a rusted machete, but it's deadly enough to cut Matt in two.

Before Matt can crack a smile, Silver throws herself into his arms. It's even better than he remembers. The feel of her. The solid feel of her weight pushing against his. There is nothing better. He wraps his arms around her waist and holds on. There is no need to let go. Ever again.

Matt buries his face in her hair. She smells like the forest.

Dirt and blood and grime and fear. But there is the faint scent of her citrusy shampoo beneath it all. Feeling a burst of courage, he plants a kiss on her cheek, catching the corner of her mouth.

Silver pulls back, holds him at arms' length, her gaze roaming over his face, over his toned arms. But they are nothing like the bulk's standing beside her.

"It's so good to see you," she says, causing him to blush a little under her scrutiny.

"And you." Matt squeezes her hand. "I'm so glad you made it. I heard the hellhounds were in the forest and I didn't know what to think." His gaze falls to the necklace hanging by her collarbone. The quaver pendant. The one he gave her the last time he saw her. Despite the intimidating presence of the bulk standing protectively at her side—and doesn't he know it's Matt's job to protect her? —the lightness that fills him up is like nothing he's ever experienced. It's almost like he has wings.

"Well, we had an up close and personal with one," she says, her gaze going to the bulk and drawing him into the conversation. "I'll tell you about it later."

Silver met a hellhound?

Matt faces the bulk, tries not to let the fact that the guy is a foot and a half taller than him bother him. *Tries* being the operative word. But how can he compete with a guy who's a good couple of years older, looks like he's been pumping iron since he burst out of the womb, and won't stop looking at Silver like she's...dessert.

"Matt, this is Joe. We met in the woods and he saved me, more than once."

Matt winces against the tenderness in her tone. A burning sensation fills his throat. Should he have told her under the willow tree? About his feelings? About how much he loves her? Is it now too late?

Gritting his teeth, Matt offers a hand to Joe. Recognition kicks in. He is the football player who got dropped during his first season because of a busted knee. Denied a regeneration nanite. Matt can't see anything about him that looks busted. But beneath that armored skin, who knows?

Joe shakes his hand, his grip firm, but Matt knows it could be a hell of a lot firmer. Joe could break his hand with one shake if he wanted to.

Matt glances at the ridge line, still hoping it's not just the two of them. "Where's your dad?" Silver deflates. Her entire body crumples in on itself. Joe's body tenses too, all the muscles in his corded frame coiling tight. "Shit. Is he...?"

"He was injured during the hellhound attack," Silver says. "And captured."

Matt doesn't know what to say. The shock is a punch to the guts. Not just because it's Rufus, the guy who saved his life, the friend of his parents he's known all his life, the scientist who the resistance is pinning all their hopes on. But because it's Silver that matters right now. Her dad has been captured. Her mom is in prison. She is alone.

"Taken by the army." Shadows loom under Silver's eyes. She's clearly been to hell and back. More than once. Matt squeezes her hand again.

Silver made it to the cave. That's what matters now. Lyla is in a compound. More people arrive every day, putting a strain on their resources. If they have to rescue Lyla and

Rufus, then that's what they'll do. They are together now. Nothing will part them again. Whatever battles are in their future, they will fight them together.

As best friends. Because that's what they have always been. There is no reason to complicate things now. Matt would take a bullet for Silver and he knows she would do the same. That is all that matters. He can face anything with Silver by his side.

⋊⋉⋊⋉

Thank you so much for making it all the way to the end. I hope you have enjoyed seeing things from Matt's point of view in this companion novella and are excited to discover the rest of the series. If you did, leaving a review is the best possible present for an author! You can do it here:

https://geni.us/MattLawson

Grap the next instalment, Joe Rucker, here...

https://geni.us/JoeRucker

FACEBOOK READERS GROUP

If you want to experience more of my books, do join my Facebook readers group where you can chat to other readers and discuss my books, as well as anything else you are reading. I am very active in this group, and you can expect book jokes, puzzles, riddles, quizzes, giveaways, the opportunity to name characters, as well as secret information about what I'm working on, cover reveals and so much more!

Just click here: https://www.facebook.com/groups/840324970233576

If you'd like to read the next book in the series for FREE, please sign up to my newsletter at

https://www.marisanoelle.com/subscribe/

And don't forget there are 10 more companion novellas in the series:

Silver Melody
Joe Rucker
Paige Starling
Hal Small
Erica Swiftfield
Kyle Lewis
Jacob Shea
Sawyer Watson
Addison Shields
President Bear